Ten Thousand walks

A Legend Is Born

BY: William D. Ollivierre

Cover art by: William D. Ollivierre

A MOW Universe Publishing Production
Published by William D. Ollivierre

ISBN: 978-1-7359149-1-6

MOW Universe

Mow Universe is the brainchild of William Ollivierre years in the making, now coming to the public. This is the first of the MOW Universe books a collection of a few short stories from MOW that spread across both space and time to allow you to see as much of MOW as possible in as little time as possible.
Mow can be found online at
http://mowuniverse.com

I would like to thank God for bringing me from a ten-year-old child that could barely read or write, to allowing me to finish and publish book after book.

Also, thank my family and friends for all the support, I wouldn't be writing without it.

Last special thanks to Emoni McGregor for all the help getting this book ready.

For all those who need an escape from reality.
Come escape with me.

<u>Intro</u>

They are people throughout history that stand and cast a shadow on evrything and everyone around them.
They leave a mark on the world around them for good and sometimes for evil, as their names become a thing of legend known to all.

Now enter a universe where the words Ten Thousand echoes through every planet, moon, and star system, bring hope to those that are hopeless.
While instilling fear in the hearts of those that are evil and ruthless.
This tale tells the journey of what it takes Daniel to go from a regular unheard-of explorer to become the most powerful legend in the universe.

Table of Contents

Table of Contents

Ten Thousand Walks

A Legend Is Born

BY: William D. Ollivierre

Act I

Chapter 1: The Realization

Ten Thousand Walks

Many eons ago when time itself was still new, a curse of life was placed on a man. This man was so full of pride and greed that he thought himself to be above God himself. He felt that everything that had ever gone wrong in his life was God trying to keep him down. He was so conceited and full of himself that he thought he should be the one to rule the entire universe, he was so consumed by this thought that he set out on a path to do just that. Waging war against the entire world but unfortunately, this war led to the destruction of most of the world, and what little of the world wasn't destroyed was left as a dying wasteland. His ego knew no bounds, even after all the destruction he had caused he still felt himself above everyone else. As bleak as this seemed there was a ray of hope, in his quest to become supreme ruler he had poisoned the world and, in the process, poisoned himself.

Within a year of the war he started ending, he was on his deathbed, he cursed God and all of creation with his last breath in a feeble show of power. This, however, was his final and biggest mistake, instead of dying God dealt him a curse worse than death. Forever trapping him in his dying body, to forever be in pain on the brink of death but never feeling the relief of death. He would be forced to rebuild the world he destroyed, then forever fix the mistakes of man in the shadows of history. However, as

A Legend Is Born

interesting as his story is this is not that story. This story is about that poor soul's first-born son, Daniel.

He grew up like any other typical boy with nothing out of the ordinary, going to school and having friends, getting in trouble like normal boys. His father had hidden his past from him and did his best to give Daniel a normal life. Soon the boy grew into a man of great character due to the teachings of his father. Intelligent and kind, always helping those around him, with a very wild side, and a thirst for adventure, always exploring and seeking out new things to do and learn, was just a small part of what made him great.

As he grew older, time began to show him that he was different from the people around him. This was made evident on his fiftieth birthday. When a party was thrown for him by one of his childhood classmates, which he hadn't seen in years. The day of the party arrived, Daniel was filled with anticipation as he approached the room the party was going to be held in.

Years had passed since the last time he had seen any of his friends from school, and he was greatly looking forward to seeing what they had done with their lives. As he walked into the room, he was meet with complete silence. He was a man appearing to be in his early twenties walking into a room filled with people who looked as if they could be his parents and even grandparents in some cases. Everyone was shocked by what they were seeing. Daniel looked the same as he did when they had last seen him. Which for many was more than thirty-five years ago. As he looked around the room of what seem to be old folks at that moment, he knew the feeling of being different he had always felt wasn't just a feeling in the back of his mind, but he indeed was something different.

His mind started to wonder as he began to realize the reason he had felt different his whole life, his mind began to think of all the moments in his life where he was completely different from everyone else, but his thoughts were interrupted as his best friend from school walked up to him. *"Wow, we all knew you were different, but man we didn't think you were that different. Come on tell us your secret how do you stay looking so young?"* His friend said to him laughing and pushing him more into the room with everyone else. *"Come on have a little fun why don't you, it your birthday so enjoy the party with us."*

Daniel walked around the party talking and greeting everyone as he went, but his mind wasn't there and the few hours the party lasted seemed to go by like a blink of an eye to Daniel. His thoughts had consumed him completely as he began to see how he had spent his life, from the time he left the small city he grew up in it was all

A Legend Is Born

exploring and learning from then on. He had wasted no time with anything else so much so that he never noticed the people around him aging while he stayed the same. He didn't even realize how long it had been since he left school and started his little quest for knowledge.

It didn't make sense how could he have not noticed all around him aging while he stayed the same. After all, he had seen people on his journey more than once, then the realization that the only person he had seen regularly was his father who hadn't change either. Which in itself is very unusual, his father would just show up from time to time without warning. Something anyone else would have found strange, but he never questioned it once. The fact that he had been cut off from everyone else more than thirty-five years started to set in. He knew that his family was different, they aged much slower than everyone else around them but he didn't know the reason why. He left the party with only one thought to find out the truth from his father.

As he thought about the questions he was going to ask his father, he wandered aimlessly through the city. He had to know what it was that made him this way, and what else his father was keeping from him. There is just one problem; he had no idea how to find his father. In the past, his father had always found him from time to time unexpectedly. But he had never actually set out to find him and found him before. This didn't stop him from setting out to find him, and so he set out on what was going to be the most important quest of his life or so he thought. With a mind full of questions, he journeyed across the lands in search of his father. Day after day he searched but nothing. The days quickly turned into years as he sought out his father, growing more frustrated by the day. The many times, he had seen his father before he had never had to search for him, yet he always popped up every few months. Now looking every place, he could think to look he still found nothing.

Nevertheless, he continued to look; year after year, he searched. He had to know what made him and his father different. What was unique about them, and was it just the two of them? What about his mother is this the reason he had never meet her? The search continued growing more dangerous with each passing day. He began to faced mortal danger the likes of which he had never encountered in all his years of exploring. It was as if the universe was trying to stop him from finding his father at any cost. Danger was at every turn he made, bring him within inches of death time after time, but every time he would survive against all the odds. For 150 years, he searched high and low for his father, losing track of time

A Legend Is Born

and even forgetting who he was looking for, getting caught up by the wonders of the world while searching.

The day before his 200th birthday came without him even realizing. He stopped in a valley and took a day to himself to celebrate and relax. He laid in the tall, soft grass of the valley, wind on his face and the rays of the sun hitting his face. *"Ahh today is such a perfect day there is no possible way this could be any nicer."* He said to himself then closed his eyes as the clouds strolled across the blue skies above him. The thought that it would be the perfect gift for his father to show up and answer his questions came and went with a smile.

Even though he had been looking for his father for such a long time, he knew he had not even covered half of the world yet. Searching the world on foot for a person was a very time-consuming task, and no matter how fast he tried to move it was never fast enough. He would always have to stop for some reason, rumors of his father being nearby, people who said they knew his location and helping those that were in danger. Making it seem as if his father was always one step away from him just at the next city looking back at him hiding from his sight. Leaving a trail for him to follow endlessly around the world, making him feel like a kite on a string, floating in the wind but still tethered to the ground.

A Legend Is Born

Ten Thousand Walks

As his thoughts wandered, he began to think it was time for him to give up on his father and just think about himself. He would find the answers he wanted on his own or not at all. He didn't care either way, he just wanted the endless search to be over with. His eyes opened with the thought of going on with his life. However, he was pleased with what he saw.

He saw a figure above him, and as the face came into focus, he saw his father's face floating above him. He couldn't help but to start laughing. *"I must really be tired of searching if I'm starting to see things now."* He said as he continued to laugh. *"Really, what are you seeing?"* Replayed his father, Daniel jumped up to find his father was actually real and standing right before him.

"No this isn't fair, this can't be real, you can't be real. After all this time it just can't be happening like this." Daniel said to his father, a bit annoyed. His father just looked at him with a smile. *"I thought you wanted to find me and have a chat with your dear old dad. So why are you upset now that I'm right here in front of you?"* His father said as he helped him to his feet. *"Really? I should be happy to see you when I've been searching for you for the last 150 years and you just happen to show up when I'm done searching for you."* Daniel said getting more annoyed as he spoke.

A Legend Is Born

Ten Thousand Walks

Though he was upset, he was still thrilled to see his father after so long. More importantly, he had a lot of questions for him, but his father wanted to catch up first. So, they spent the rest of the afternoon and all of the night catching up. They shared all the new adventures they went on over the years they hadn't seen each other. His father even told him how he stayed close by to him the whole time. Something that Daniel didn't want to hear, even more so when he found out that they were always in the same city. His father seemed to have been leading him around the world dropping clues to keep him following him all these years. Not only that but, the times his son was seriously injured, he would show up, dress, and clean the wounds without him knowing and leave. Leaving him in the same place so he would think it was his own doing. The conviction made Daniel mad, but at the same time, it made him feel as though his search wasn't a total waste of time seeing that his father was with him watching over him the whole time.

They talked and talked, catching up on all the things in their lives and what they were planning on doing over the next few years. Before they knew it, the sun was starting to peak its head over the horizon. Daniel's father looked at him and gestured for him to follow him as they walked out of the valley they were in the night before. His father's expression changed from a fun mood to a serious one, he was about to tell him something very important. Daniel waited with great anticipation maybe his father was finally going to start answering his questions.

What happened next caught Daniel entirely off guard. *"My son, you are now 200 years old, and by now I would assume that you have figured out that you age much slower than everyone around you, and for some reason, you can survive a lot more than a normal human can."* Said Carlton to Daniel, who was left speechless by what his father had just said. It was as if he took the words right out of his mind; after a few seconds of speechlessness, he spoke. *"Yes, I have noticed that it was the reason I started searching for you, and it's the reason I kept searching for so long, I need to know why I am like this. I need to know what makes me so different from everyone else."* Daniel Said.

Carlton smiled at his son, and then he turned his face to the sun as it slowly and lazily lifted itself higher into the sky, almost as if it didn't want to be climbing into the skies. *"Well, as I watched you at your birthday party I realized that you were starting to feel different from everyone else. I knew then that you needed to know the truth about what you are, but I didn't just want to go out and tell you everything, and you not believe me. So, I headed off right*

A Legend Is Born

Ten Thousand Walks

in front of you making sure to stay just a step in front of you, also making sure you followed the path I set for you. Then I made sure to keep pushing you past your limits as much as I could without having you think I was the one setting you up." Carlton said as he slowly walked to the center of the valley as if searching for something. His son followed close behind him looking around to see what he was looking for. Carlton stopped and bent down to one knee, then he started to move his hands through the grass looking for something. Daniel looked at him, wondering what he was looking for. He had come to this valley many times before on his journey looking for his father, but he had never seen anything out of the ordinary here.

Click. A sound came from under the grass. *"There it is, let's finish talking inside. I know you may not remember playing in my lab when you were just a little boy, after all, it was a very long ago."* Carlton said as he stood to his feet. The ground under them began to move apart, opening up to a stairway that led down into a dark room.

Carlton stepped down first. His feet touched the first step, and as it did the room light up. Daniel followed slowly after his father, stepping down into the lab, as he looked around, he could remember playing around the tables and with the odd devices that were on the tables. However, that was where his memories ended. His father looked back with a smile on his face as they walked. *"You remember now don't you, I haven't been to this one since the last time we were both in here. That's why I brought you to this lab instead of any of the others. it's the last place we were both truly ourselves."* Said Carlton, as he walked over to one of the desks in the lab.

"Come, my boy sit with me, and I'll explain everything to you." Said Carlton to Daniel as he sat in a nearby chair, gesturing for Danielle to sit in the chair across from him. Daniel sat in the chair that was across from his father and looked around. He thought back to his childhood, and all the time he spent in the lab, but for some reason, he didn't remember the lab being so huge. He couldn't even see the walls as he looked around. He did, however, remember the table he was sitting at, it was the same one he would sit at and play every time he was in the lab.

Carlton leaned back in the chair and relaxed, he closed his eyes and with a smile began to speak. *"50,000 years ago, I was a well-known and brilliant scientist. I worked hard day and night on my greatest invention. It took me years, but I did it, and I was proud of it, so much so in fact that I tried to use it to take over the world. However, in my arrogance, I almost destroyed the earth and all life on this planet. Luckily, my plans failed, and I was left sick and dying, yet still, I didn't admit that I was at fault. Even* in my mind I still felt as if it was my right to be a ruler and I did nothing wrong. Because of this, I cursed God on my deathbed. I blamed God for all I had done wrong, and for all the destruction, pain, and sickness. I had caused. Then I took my last breath, only to have it and my soul pushed right back into my body. Then cursed with never-ending life by God as punishment for what I had done. Which at first thought made me feel like I was the one doing the punishing, I felt as if I was making God give me never-ending life. However, the truth about the curse was felt as my pain grew. I was in a body that would never die, but would still age and get sick, and if that wasn't enough, I had to undo the damage I had done to the earth or grow even sicker."

Daniel only looked on at his father wondering why he was not told about all of this much earlier. *"I know you must be wondering right about now why I have never told you about the curse. It's not that I was hiding it from you but more that I just wanted you to be old enough to understand how lonely it is to have everything you care about fade all around you. Something your mother couldn't handle and decided to leave before you could remember her so you wouldn't have to watch her grow old and die as I did. It wasn't just that I also had to be absolutely sure you were cursed as I was before I told you* about it. Once I was sure I came up with this long trip in order to prove everything I am telling you now, after all being told You will live forever and nothing will ever be able to kill you isn't easy to believe." Carlton said with a sad smile.

Daniel jumped up from the chair a thousand thoughts running through his mind. "So that's why I age so slowly and why I can survive all hell breaking loose. I knew I was different I just knew it, but I would have never guessed that I was immortal this is awesome!" Daniel said with excitement, as his father sat across from him calmly smiling. Carlton realized that his son did not fully understand why this was a curse mainly because his son was much too young to understand. Even so, he knew it was still the best choice that he tell him now before he figured it out on his own. However, for now, it was his birthday, and he was going to let him enjoy it as much as possible. After all, he would soon begin to hate them as time passed and each one reminded him of the life he had.

Once Daniel and his father finish talking they headed back up to the surface. The opening in the ground closed back as the two walked back into the valley. "Well, I know I just dropped a lot on you, but I must go. It seems as though I am needed elsewhere, Humans are so needy sometimes. Hope you enjoy the rest of your birthday, after all, you only

A Legend Is Born

turn 200 once." Carlton said with a smile on his face then walked off into the valley and soon vanished from sight.

Daniel watched as his father faded in the distance, he didn't really care where his father was going off to or what he meant by needy Humans. He was just too overwhelmed and lost in the news he had just gotten, he felt like an entirely new man in a completely new body. Although he knew he was different before, and that nothing had actually changed, he felt as if he was just given an entirely new life. Nothing had changed yet somehow it felt as if everything had changed, that odd feeling of not fitting in, the feeling of being different his entire life, it all started to make sense now. As he continued to think about his new life, he began to walk out of the valley; his mind wondered about what his dad told him, and how his life was a cursed one, but he thought that part must be a joke.

Soon he was walking alongside a clear blue river. As he did, he turned and gazed into the flowing waters, he smiled at his reflection as he thought this could not possibly be a curse. This wasn't a curse this was the greatest gift anyone had ever given or would ever give him. He could do anything and everything he had ever thought of doing no matter how dangerous it was or how long it would take him to do.

Daniel's mind overflowed with possibilities, as the

Ten Thousand Walks

realization of never-ending life finally set in. His mind quickly filled up with all the things he wanted to do but never had time to do. However, now he had all the time in the universe to do everything and anything he could ever think of doing. He sat on the bank of the river, staring at his shimmering reflection. Knowing he could do all the things he had ever wanted to do made him very excited for his future. However, for the time being, he just wanted to relax and enjoy the moment, before he set out on any new journey.

A Legend Is Born

Chapter 2: The Journey Begins

"Yesterday I turned 200 years old, and it was by far the best birthday, I have ever had. Not only did I get to meet my father after so many years. I was also given the greatest gift I could ever be given. After finding out the truth, I felt like a completely different person, as if I was given a pass to a brand-new life. Starting today, I am going to live every day like never before. But first I should really stop talking to myself, I can't believe I still hold conversions with myself after 120 years of telling myself that I won't do it anymore." Said Daniel to himself sitting up on the river bank, he had fallen asleep on the river's edge the night before while thinking about all the things he wanted to accomplish.

He looked down at his reflection in the water, took a deep breath, and began thinking about where he would go from this point. He then reached out and touched the water with the tips of his fingers, then moved them across his reflection slowly, doing his best not to ripple his reflection. *"Hmm, so where do you think we should go today handsome?"* He asked his reflection with a big smile on his face, then swiped his fingers across the surface of the water quickly, distorting the bottom of his reflection but not his face. Then, with an enormous grin on his face, he stood to his feet, looking in every direction as he decided which way he would be heading off too. North, he thought that would be the best use of his time.

"Wait a Sec, I am never going to die, time no longer matters so what am I thinking about right now. I need to be thinking of where I really want to go. Not what time will allow for." His words changed his trend of thought as he went from thinking of the closet and best use of his time to thinking about all the amazing things he had heard of, all the fantastic things he never had time to see, and all the amazing things he had seen before.

There were so many amazing places that he had seen in his travels over the past century and a half searching for his father, but even after all that time, there was still so much that he hadn't seen. All the legends that he had come across that told of wondrous places and people; that defied logic and would give you an entirely new meaning to what it is to be human, they held beauty and wonders in ways that not even the words could express. He wanted to see them all, but now the big choice he would be facing was what he wanted to see first, and which direction he should head off to in order to start his great journey.

He lifted his head high to the deep blue skies, then

leaned back and fell into the river behind him with a giant splash. He took his time to enjoy the water, surfacing about a minute later, shaking his head, and then he began to run his hands through his hair as he spoke aloud to himself. *"That was exactly what I needed on such a hot day like today. Now my mind is cleared, I'll be able to figure out exactly what I need to do."* He smiled as he drifted down the river, letting the water carry him slowly downstream towards the River's end, which should be leading to open ocean. *"I've got it, I know exactly what I want to do first! I am going to jump off every waterfall I have ever heard of and hopefully find some new ones that no one's ever heard of. That should take me most of the summer if not the whole thing, which means once the summer is over I should have seen every waterfall on the planet. Then I'll find something else to do for the winter, after all, it would be too cold to jump off a waterfall in the winter anyway."* Daniel said as he drifted down the River.

Oddly enough, the river Daniel was floating down did not let out at the ocean. Instead, its mouth was a waterfall, known as God's Mouth. It is the second largest waterfall on the planet; soaring into the skies about a thousand feet from bottom to top. This extreme height was due to a 300-foot deep cave that the waterfall fell directly into. This of course was common knowledge to everyone. What was not common knowledge, however, was what was on the bottom of the waterfall. Which was a secret society unknown to the world for hundreds of years. This was all going to change as this secret society was about to meet an outsider like no other.

Daniel heard the rushing waters in the distance and knew instantly what it meant. There was a waterfall close by, and based on the last place he was, he knew it could only be one waterfall. An eager grin came across his face, he was going to start seeing the magnificent waterfalls of the world a lot sooner than he had expected, and he was going to start with one of the biggest in the world. The timing of this couldn't be any better if he had planted it himself, then a momentary passing thought came to his mind. Maybe it was planned, perhaps that's why his father had led him to this place, so he could see this waterfall for his birthday.

He smiled as he began to swim faster towards the mouth of the waterfall; the water around him began to flow quicker caring him along even faster than he could swim. Soon he was no longer swimming. Instead, he was just staying afloat as the rushing waters of the river pulled him towards the edge. The sound of the waterfall grew with each passing second, and soon the sound of the rushing water became a roar. The sound filled the atmosphere, shaking and vibrating everything around the waterfall. He could feel the vibrations going down his spine, sending tingles through his entire body. His heartbeat grew faster his palms clenched, and his eyes grew wider, all in anticipation of the fall.

He grabbed onto the straps of the bag he was wearing, pulling it close to his back, then braced himself for the fall. He could see the rushing waters falling over the side, and as dangerous, as it looked, it was also beautiful at the same time. The mist from the water flowed like a cloud over the edge and back up again. Making the deadly rushing water look like a soft cloud slowly overflowing and floating down the side of the cliff into the cave below. Daniel knew better, he knew that the cloud of beauty that was hiding the waterfall was only formed on the deadliest of waterfalls. As the thought ran through his mind, his faced changed. This was going to be the most spectacular moment of his life thus far. The grin on his face went from ear to ear as he went into the cloud. Moments later, he was going over the edge. There was no turning back now.

Over he went. Falling through the air and water was like nothing he had felt. The sound of the water was different than he expected. It was as if every time the water hit the back of the waterfall, it made the sound of a footstep. With so much water hitting behind him it sounded as though there was an army of unimaginable size marching behind his head. Then there was the sound of the water moving through the air, which was like a beautiful song being sung by a thousand singers. It was a peaceful song, yet it was so loud that he could feel it echoing through his very being. As he looked, around he could see the water around him slow down the faster he fell until the water came to a stop as they both were falling at the same speed. The ice-cold water soon engulfed him as he passed through the opening of the cave mouth, he would be at the bottom soon.

He closed his eyes as he slowly exhaled, letting the sounds of the water and the feeling of the cold droplets on his skin fill his every thought. Then allowing his mind wander off, not worrying about what would happen next just existing in that one moment in time. It was a fantastic feeling, as time seemed to be standing still, seconds turned into hours, and the moment seemed to fill his very soul. It was a feeling he never felt before, it was the first time in his life he had really stopped to enjoy the moment.

But unfortunately, as much as he would like it to, time stands still for no one, not even one that's immortal. The songs of the water quickly changed, the calming melody of the water was replaced by the crushing boom of the water colliding with the bottom. The bottom of the waterfall was now inches away from him. He opened his eyes to the pitch-black cave. Then in an instant, the water quickly turned on him.

Slamming his body into the water below with crushing force then, pounded him deep into the depths of the icy frozen waters. He struggled to swim up and forward out of the crushing water's path, but it was useless the water's forces was just too much for anyone to overcome. It pushed on him harder and harder, pushing him deeper and deeper. Before he knew it, he was slammed against the rocky bottom of the lake below the waterfall. Then it all went dark, his body began to twist out of shape as the crushing force of the water pounded him more and more into the lakes rocky bed.

Out of nowhere, a rope drifted down and wrapped around his right leg then tightened. It slowly began to pull him out of the crushing force of the water, it took almost a full minute, and by the time his body was out of the water, it was mangled and bloody. It seemed hopeless as the water around his body turned red as the blood could be seen pouring from every inch of his body. His bloody body was slowly pulled towards the edge of the lake.

The person pulling his body from the lake could not be seen in the darkness, but whoever it was had to be strong. If Daniel actually survives this and wakes up any time soon, he was going to be in for a huge surprise. To find that there were people actually living at the bottom of the waterfall.

Ten Thousand Walks

Act II

Chapter 3: The Awakening

Ten Thousand Walks

Daniel's mangled and bloody body was pulled from the lake by a few of the natives that lived on the lake's edge. He was alive, but barely breathing, and blood could be seen pouring from every inch of his body. The natives quickly and carefully wrapped his body in bandages to slow the bleeding. Then very carefully picked him up, and carried him to what looked like a hut of some kind.

Inside of the hut like structure was dimly lit by a blue glow that was radiating from lines running up the sides of the walls. The lines meet at an orb-like mirror in the ceiling, which was then reflecting the light down and out, splitting the light into soft rays of green and purple as a reflected it down onto the ground.

The natives surrounded him on all sides. They were very short people just about 4 feet tall, but this wasn't what stood out most about them. What stood out the most was their eyes. There was an ever so subtle, but bright glow in their eyes. Looking at them at first you wouldn't be able to tell, but it was there. It was a bright green glow yet it was so subtle it was almost unseen. The glow came from the white in their eyes, making it seem as though Daniel's body was surrounded by glowing green rings floated in midair.

They sat around Daniel in a circle, then they started placing medicines of all kinds on his body as they slowly placed his bones back in place. Once they finish setting his bones in place and putting splints on them, they began to rub his body with a yellow paste that was made of herbs. Moments after the wounds on his body began to smoke, a yellow mist rose from his body as the herb seemed to just sink into his skin. The yellow herbs vanished from his skin, then his wounds began to heal, his skin pulled itself back together and as the gashes touched the cuts disappeared from them. Even his bones could be heard healing themselves as they cracked straightening out. The properties of the strange medicine they were using were just amazing, not only did it speed his healing rate up by almost one hundred times, but it also made his body heal as though it had never been hurt in the first place.

Then suddenly his body began to tense up, his eyes opened, and he slowly began to regain consciousness. The medicine was burning his body, making him feel as though he was on fire, forcing him to awaken as his wounds finish closing. Daniel began to scream out in pain, even though he was no longer bleeding his body felt as though it was being burnt from the inside. He continued to scream for a few minutes. As the smoke coming from the medicine slowly began to dissipate, his screams gradually lessened. The scars that had formed a few minutes earlier soon disappeared. The smoke stopped entirely and with it so did the pain, soon Daniel screams stopped as he lost consciousness once again.

Daniel remained unconscious at this point. More than two weeks past as he slept. Constantly being watched over by one of the villages, who were taking turns making sure his bandages with a green-blue paste on it was changed daily. A very odd thing to be doing considering his body had already healed. However, it turned out this paste wasn't medicine like the yellow one, this was a form of life support. The paste absorbed into his body given him the necessary nutrients needed to stay alive. After the first week of him sleeping, the villages began to move him every morning, they took him to the edge of the village to a calm spot in the lake.

This was where the plants they used to make the yellow medicine placed on his body was grown. They put his body in the water at the very edge of the shore, then pulled the plants all over his body wrapping him tightly with them. They left him wrapped up like this for an hour every morning. This not only cleaned his body of the life support medicine that was placed on it the day before, but it also covered his body in oil that the plants only secreted while there were still growing. The oil would help his internal organs heal even faster, it prevented his body from weakening while he was unconscious, and increased the blood flow throughout his body, preventing any side effects that go along with laying without moving for weeks. After that, they would return his body to the hut in which he was staying, changing his bandages and reapplied the medicine and herbs across his body. After that, they would leave him to continue to heal without moving him until the next morning, when they would start the whole process over again. Even though it looked as if the medicine was working miracles from the outside, it couldn't speed up the healing of his internal organs as much as his skin and bones. This moving back and forth went on every day for a few weeks before Daniel woke up.

Before his eyes could even open, he was already confused. His body was wrapped tightly in vines and almost completely submerged in water. As you might assume this isn't the best way for anyone to wake up. He felt angry and scared at the same time wondering what had happened to him, and wondering how he ended up in this position. His eyes opened slowly, the place he was laying was dimly lit, with just enough light for everything to be seen semi-clearly.

As his eyes adjusted and the environment became clear he could tell that he wasn't outside or at least not outside as he was used to. There was no sky, and all he could see was a rocky surface above his head. It took a little while for him to completely wake up and for his mind to clear enough for him to realize where he was. He was in a cave. However, it was very odd, he thought, if he was in a cave, it should be dark, but he could see clearly though it wasn't as bright as being outside it still had more than enough light for him to see clearly. He looked around thinking that he was close to the entrance of the cave after all, it was too bright for him to be very far inside. However, as far as his eyes could see, there were no entrances, and no light coming in from anywhere. Then again, he could only see what was above him seeing that he couldn't move his head or the rest of his body.

The villager that was supposed to be in charge of looking after him at the moment didn't even notice he had regained consciousness because of how little he could move. The villager was expecting him to start panicking immediately if he was to regain consciousness. However, Daniel was laying perfectly still and perfectly calm, well more like dazed and confused to the point where he didn't realize he wasn't trying to get free. Even though he was panicking, he wasn't moving or trying to get free he was just screaming out in his mind wondering what's going on.

After coming to his senses Daniel actually started to panic, he immediately tried to jump up and ripped the vines of his body. However, this was not happening as he saw it in his mind, his body just laid there not responding to his commands all except for the pinky on his right hand. Which is very odd because he was left-handed. It took almost ten minutes of him trying to scream and utterly failing at making even one sound before the villager noticed that he was awake after she saw his eyes blinking.

The villager quickly, yet very carefully removed the vines from across Daniel's body. Then slowly pulled him out of the water onto the shore next to the bed they used to carry him back and forth. Then she quickly ran off to go find the other villagers. She returned about three minutes later with two more villagers to help carry Daniel back to the hut. They moved him to the bed and carried him back to the Hut, he couldn't do anything but move his pinky and his head slightly to the side. He was amazed by what he saw as they carried him quickly back to the hut and set him down in the middle directly under the orb.

Daniel laid in the hut, wondering where he was, who these people were, and what had actually happened to him. Oddly enough, it didn't occur to him to think about how much time had actually passed since he was last awake. His mind had already adapted to the fact that he was an immortal, though it was a short amount of time since he had found out that he was. He had adapted so much that the passage of time no longer occurred to him.

Ten Thousand Walks

However, this was just because he was out for so long and his mind had the time to absorb what his father had said as he slept.

Nevertheless, like any sane person who had been asleep for a very long time, and waking up in a strange place surrounded by very strange people, he was scared and confused. However, he figured there wasn't very much for him to be worrying about, after all, they dressed his wounds and were taking excellent care of him. He just hoped that they actually spoke a language he could understand, that way he would be able to thank them for their help. Hopefully keeping any misunderstandings from happening, or keeping the ones that occurred to a minimum. Which might be a bit hard to do considering that he wasn't very good at getting along with people.

A Legend Is Born

Chapter 4: The Cave Dwellers

Daniel laid in the center of a small hut. Interested
villages packed themselves into the hut one after the
next until there was no room to move, then the squeezed
them self in some more packing themselves till they could
barely take a breath. Daniel was the first outsider any of
the villagers had ever seen. However, that wasn't the main
reason they were all surrounding him. The reason for this
intense interest was the that he had actually survived the
fall, even though he was severely injured in it, he was still
alive.

Daniel's eyes moved around the room as he tried
to move his head with little success. His eyes were soon
drawn to a villager that looked different from all the rest.
She must be the village leader he thought as he looked
her up and down. His mouth trembled as he tried to make
words come out, but not even a single sound came out of
his mouth. All he could do was just watch in silence, even
with no success he continued to try and get her attention.
Then she seemed to understand him, well that was his first
thought, but she turned and started telling a few of the
villages something. He didn't hear her say anything, but
he knew she did when they quickly left and brought back

a small bowl filled with a green, yellow, and brown paste. They mixed it around until it became one black color, after which they added water from a different bowl, put it to his mouth and slowly fed it to him.

The village leader moved closer to him, she smiled, then spoke loud enough for only him to hear. *"Come on you have to eat, you need to get your strength back before you can do anything. Don't worry, I know it tastes like it will kill you, but it won't trust me, it will have you back on your feet in no time."* She said with a reassuring smile, Daniel was shocked and confused at the same time by the village leader, not by what she had said, but by the fact that he could understand her perfectly, but it was the language she was speaking and not that he could understand what she was saying that shocked him.

The langue she was speaking was not common, it was so uncommon he had only heard it spoken by one other person during his entire life, his father. As a child, he learned to speak this language, with his father insisting he learn it perfectly. A very odd thing considering his father also told him the langue was a dead language. Nevertheless, he picked it up quite easily seeing that his father spoke it more than he spoke any other langue.

As Daniel forced himself to swallow the horrible tasting paste, he thought that he must have been hearing things when the village leader spoke to him. She couldn't have been speaking the language he thought she was. However, as the silence in the room was broken by the villagers speaking amongst themselves, he realized that they were speaking the same language. This just brought even more questions to his mind and made him even more confused about the villagers.

Within an hour of drinking the black death tasting liquid, he was able to sit up and speak softly. *"Hello, my name is Daniel, thank you for taking care of me. Can I ask where I am and who you are? Also, how did I get here?"* The villagers were shocked and amazed, not only by the fact that he had healed enough to sit up and speak, but also that he spoke their language. *"How is it possible that you can speak our language when you have never been here?"* Asked the village leader in a surprised and confused tone.

"I learned to speak it as a small child. It was the only thing my father spoke at home." Replied Daniel, the chief looked at him with disbelief and surprised. Then after pausing for a few minutes, she began to speak again. *"Well, we haven't had contact with the outside world in what seems like forever."* She paused for a few seconds, then continued. *"Your father wouldn't happen to be Carlton, would he?"* Asked the chief with a very skeptical

voice.

"*Yes, he is my father, and to answer your next question, yes, he is that old.*" Replied Daniel, surprising even himself by the words he was speaking. The chief just laughed, Daniel looked around and could see most of the villages in the hut were actually smiling too. "*We all know how old he is, he is the person responsible for our home here. If it weren't for him, we would all be living on the surface right now. But we never thought that the cursed one would have kids. Actually, we didn't think he could have kids.*" She said happily and then looked him up and down for a while. "*It's a good thing that he was able to have children, from what I was told as a child he seemed like a very lonely person. So how old would you be Daniel.*" She said very eager to find out the answer.

Daniel looked at her with confusion, then tried to answer her while stumbling over his words. "*I... well umm, 200 years old, how do you.*" Daniel stopped for a second; he knew he sounded like a complete moron. He took a deep breath collected his thoughts and tried it again. "*Sorry about that, I'm 200 years old it was my birthday the day before I fell down the waterfall. But what I really want to know is how you know about my father and our curse?*" Daniel was extremely confused, even more than when he had just woken up. Everything that was happening was just

A Legend Is Born

raising more questions in his head, and he wondered what surprise was going to be next.

"It's simple really. He saved us all and brought our people here when the Great War ended. The world was left in pieces, famine and disease were spreading through the world and rumors of new wars were all that anyone talked about. Then he came bringing us together from all over the world, then bringing us here where it was safe. He taught us to live off the land, using every resource efficiently, without wasting, and without causing damage to the environment. The best part was we even ended up with more than we could use. He is even the reason for the green glow in our eyes, caused by the plants he gave us to keep us healthy and to give us a longer lifespan." She explained with a smile.

Until this moment, Daniel had no idea what his father had done after he was cursed. The people in this village were what his father had protected from his time. They had advanced technology that he had only seen in his father's lab before now. Not just that, but they seem much more peaceful than anyone he had ever seen. As a few of the villages helped him up and took him outside of the hut, he thought about his journey. Though it had just started, he had learned more about his father than he had himself, a thought that push another thought into his head, that he was never going to get away from his father's control into his mind. He had just basically fallen off the planet and yet he was still in his father's shadow. Which wasn't an awful thing, but for going on an adventure of a lifetime, it made him feel as if he was still following his father's plans.

He looked around the village as the thoughts filled his mind, taking a deep slow breath. *"You know what, this is my adventure, and I don't care what my father did a long time ago. This is my time, and I'm going to enjoy it."* Daniel said softly to himself, then smiled at the villagers that were helping him along.

As he looked around where he was and out into the village, he couldn't help but wonder how on earth did his father manage to build a city all the way down here, not only that but how did he get all these people here without killing them all on the way down. The questions on how this wondrous city came to be filled his mind as he took in the sheer amazement that this place was. Never before had he seen such an amazing place. It wasn't just the city in such an odd location, but it was the cave itself to. The waterfall fell into the cave in front of him bringing with it the light from the outside world, it looked as if it wasn't just water but also a waterfall of light falling into the cave. From there the light reflected off the crystal blue water like a mirror. Fulling the whole cave with a soft glow, that

A Legend Is Born

Ten Thousand Walks

rose to the roof of the cave where it looked like stars filling the sky. It was more amazing that even the night sky. Small beads of light like stars reflected off the roof in every color that was possible, creating a night like sky with stars of every color. He looked around, as his head moved the stars seemed to dance just for him changing colors and rippling across the roof.

"It's said that the ceiling of this cave was made to look like the night sky so we wouldn't miss the outside world." The villager helping to hold him up said with a smile as if he longed for a better night sky. Daniel turned to him and with a smile spoke. *"No this was not created to remind you of the outside sky, this was made so you wouldn't long for the outside. I have never seen a sky this beautiful in all my life."*

Chapter 5: God's Mouth

After walking around for a few minutes, Daniel headed back to the hut with the help of the villagers. His body was still very weak, and he wasn't able to do very much at the moment. Once back in the hut he laid back down to rest. The chief smiled at him and turned to the villagers that were still in the hut and told them to leave so that he could rest. Then, as she was getting up to leave, Daniel reached to stop her from going. *"So, tell me how is it that my father saved your people, and how long ago was this?"* Asked Daniel, she turned to him and sat back down next to him. It was calm and silent for quite a while before she looked as if she was going to answer him. She smiled as she started to speak to tell him the story of how it all started, and how they ended up beneath the waterfall. *"Just relax and I will tell you exactly what happened."* Said the chief as she got comfortable, then she began to tell the story of how they ended up under the waterfall.

The story she told started many generations ago when her people lived on the surface. *"Things were relatively peaceful back then, everyone got along just fine with everyone else. They had everything they needed, there* wasn't even any sickness or diseases. Then it happened. The first war planet Earth had ever seen. The war lasted only a few years, but in that time, it ripped the world itself into pieces. Entire cities were wiped off the face of the planet with no survivors. The forests died, the waters turn toxic, the ground turned hard, and the skies turned red. By the time the war ended, pollution from the war had utterly devastated the Earth. Those that were left over did everything they could to survive, though it was nearly impossible. They found ways of surviving on almost nothing, struggling and fighting amongst themselves just to survive.

However, not all the survivors were fighting, some of them were still trying to hold onto the peaceful life they had before the war. It was even harder for them. Then one day he just showed up out of nowhere, telling those that had decided to live in peace that he would help them. He treated the diseases they had, gave them food and water, then protected them until they regain their strength. Afterwards, he offered to take them somewhere away from everything else. My people were skeptical at first, because of the rumor that said, though he was trying to save them, he was the one that started the war in the first place. Nevertheless, they still decided to go with him even if he was the one that started the war he was making up for it now, we hoped.

He brought us to this place, the largest manufactured waterfall ever to be built. It was built for entertainment; it was something called a roller coaster. She didn't quite understand what it was, but she knew that it was made for people to enjoy themselves. They would ride it along the course of the waterfall, going down all the way then back up again. This entire cave, the river that feeds the waterfall, even the outlet at the bottom of the lake, was designed as a failsafe for the ride. However, after the war started no one went on rides anymore, and the ride was disassembled for its metals. Leaving behind this waterfall and cave, which became toxic once the war ended. When my ancestor arrived here, the waters glowed brightly in the night.

Carlton worked endlessly to clean the waters, bring in unique plants that he made to make the water clean enough to drink. Those plants gave us food and medicine also, after a few weeks the water at the bottom of the fall was clean. However, the water that fell into the lake was still toxic, but he found a way to protect us from that also. He took us to the center of the lake and built this city on the lake far enough away from the waterfall so that its toxins didn't affect us. The plants were planted around and throughout the entire city to clean the waters for us to use.

A Legend Is Born

Then he gave us more plants to heal our bodies if toxins ever got into them.

My ancestors lived here with the toxic glow of the waterfall for many generations; over that time your father visited us bring in supplies, new technology, and even more people. Though the waterfall remained toxic, no one got sick from it. Your father brought new plants every time he visited to help heal the water and us. The last time he came, he brought the plant that surrounds this island. It causes the body to heal and reject any toxins within it, though the side effect of this caused our eyes to glow. It was a small sacrifice that we happily paid to get rid of all our diseases and extend our lives by more than 100 years.

My ancestors did not live in fear of the toxic air as most of the world did at that time. Because we were underground and because of the waterfall almost completely blocking the only entrance, the poisonous air from above never made it down here to us. We think that's why your father chose this place over any other place, he could have chosen for us. Because of this, we flourished as a city, clean water, clean air, and peaceful existence with each other.

After a few generations of living beneath the surface, our records show that the water in the waterfall turned clear. No more toxins were coming into our lake and then *your father returned. He offered to take us back to the surface, to start over fresh in the New World that was above us. However, we chose to remain here, we liked it here, it is very peaceful, and it was our home. Therefore, he decided to give us the choice to leave whenever we wanted. He took those with him that wanted to leave to see the new world and left the rest of us with fresh supplies.*

Since then he has returned every few years, bringing newcomers with him, new supplies, and to make sure everything we wanted and needed was supplied. He would also take those that wanted to leave and see the world above with him. And at times, he would even increase the size of the cave so that our city could grow.

Then there is the name of this place, God's mouth. It was given that name when it was a ride before the wars began. Nevertheless, the name was almost all but forgotten after the war, though it has changed meaning since then, it still suited this place perfectly. It was no longer the ultimate ride, but instead, it was the first place with clean water, almost like the mouth of God. So, we decided to keep the name, and when some of us went to live on the surface, the name gained an entirely new meaning. The waterfall became an unchallengeable force of nature, one that no one could deify and live through.

44   *A Legend Is Born*

Ten Thousand Walks

Well, that was except for your father, he was the only person we had ever seen survive the fall until now.

Until we pulled you out of the water, we had actually thought it was him, but after seeing you survive, we knew you were related somehow. It seems as though we were right seeing that you're his son. But it is somewhat odd that you had no clue that we existed, your father really must have never told anyone that we existed down here."

The chief finish telling the story of this place, then she got up and left Daniel to rest. What she told him answered many questions about his father. Though it brought up even more questions that he wanted the answer to, it also made him see why his father was so secretive. It also made him wonder what else his father was protecting, and what else his father was keeping from him. However, for now it didn't matter, he had gotten more answers than he thought possible, so for now he was happy. He would rest and when he awoke, he would start to find his way out of this place, and continue his journey.

Ten Thousand Walks

Act III

Chapter 6: Training Begins

A Legend Is Born

Ten Thousand Walks

The village leader returned the next morning, bringing with her a change of clothes for Daniel. *"Good morning, are you up to getting out and walking around on your own today?"* She said with a smile as she put the clothes down on the ground next to his bed. *"Yes, I feel great I can't wait to get up and walk around, and see this village."* Said Daniel with a smirk on his face. She simply smiled at him and left him to change.

It didn't take long before Daniel was up, he came out of the hut and looked around. Stretching for a few minutes as he thought a little about what he was told the night before. He decided that he would walk around the city and explore a bit. He walked around the village on his own for quite some time before he met up with the village leader again. *"Hello Sir. Daniel, how are you feeling now?"* She said as she walked up next to him. *"I feel a little tired, but I'm recovering a lot better than I expected. Tell me what do I call you. Is it just chief or do you have a name that I can call you?"* Replied Daniel. She looked over at him as she walked alongside him. *"Yes, you could call me chief if you like, but my name is Sophie."* Sophie didn't say much else, but she was very excited showing Daniel around her city.

She took him to the end of the city at the end of her tour, where she showed him into a large building on the very edge of the city. Once inside there were steps that circled to the top, where they could overlook the entire city. *"I spend most of my time looking over my city, making the choices and decisions it takes to run this city, to keep everyone happy. I brought you here because I know you have more questions for me, but I actually need to get back to work. I have spent enough time walking around with you today, and not doing my work. But I do want to do as much as I can to help you, it's the least I can do to thank your father for bringing us here."* Said Sophie, as she sat down in a chair that faced the outside looking over everything. Then smiled as she began to do her work of managing the city.

As she worked, she began to speak. *"So now I'm guessing that you're wondering about how it is that your father came and went, seeing that there is no possible way he could have climbed back up the waterfall."* Sophie said as she wrote on a piece of paper. *"Actually, yes, I was just thinking about that. Looking at that waterfall, I know there's no possible way that anyone could ever climb it, especially seeing that you said he takes those who want to leave with him. So there has to be another way out of here right?"* Daniel said, hoping that she would say yes, it's over there and just points to a big door with the word exit written all over it. But he wasn't nearly that lucky.

"Yes, there it is, it's right under you at the bottom of

the lake that the city floats on." Replied Sophie, Daniel's eyes followed the waterfall down to the lake quickly. A waterfall that high would undoubtedly dig a very deep hole, which meant the bottom of the lake would be very far down. Too far down for him to actually make it without losing consciousness. Daniel realized quickly that this was the reason they had remained so isolated for generations and generations. If someone by some fantastic chance managed to get here and was still alive, there was no way for them to leave. Not only that, but there was no way for them to contact the outside world to get help from anyone.

I leaned on to one of the walls, staring at the waterfall and thinking which would be easier. Trying to get out through the bottom of the lake, which I had no idea how far down it actually went, or to climb a thousand-foot waterfall against crushing water.

"There is no possible way that I can swim to the bottom of the lake without dying." I said to her and paused for her reply, she simply looked over at me with a smirk on her face as if she had just finished laughing at something. Then I realize what she was smacking about it was what I just said. *"Well, I mean I would black out before getting to the bottom."*

Sophie didn't answer me for quite some time, she

seemed very focused on her work. *"Well yes, that would happen if you try to swim to the bottom of the lake. After all, it is over 1000 feet deep at the point where you would need to enter to get to the surface, and that's not counting the length of the cave you have to go through in order to get to the surface."* She said as she closed her books and got up from her chair. She turned to me and started to walk to the door, she had a smirk on her face that screamed I know something you don't. I quickly followed her and caught up before she could reach the door.

She turned to me. *"I want you to try and hit me as hard as you possibly can, and don't hold back because I'm a woman now. Come at me with everything you have, just let me have it as if I'm your worst enemy."* I was shocked by what she had just said. I didn't want to try to hit her, but at the same time, I didn't want to disrespect her. So, I made a fist, leaned back a little, then swung at her.

"Awww Come on, I know that's not the best you can do. I know you're still recovering, but you have to have more than that in you." She said, standing just out of my reach with a condescending smile on her face. I didn't expect her to be so fast, I thought to myself, I think I better get serious, I said to myself in my mind as I prepared to sing once again. This time I gave it everything I had, I swung with all my strength as fast as I could and as hard as

Ten Thousand Walks

I could.

It was a swing and a miss.

The third time I was determined to hit her, I pulled my right hand back and swung as hard as I could, with my left hand following right behind it in the opposite direction. This way, even if my right hand missed she would walk directly into my left. I quickly fell forward almost falling on my face, I was punching at the air. She was gone. She wasn't even in front of me anymore.

Then came a tap on my shoulder. *"There you go that was much better than your first two tries. But sadly, you can't hit me moving so slow, it's just impossible. Come follow me, I'll show you our training grounds, and you can see firsthand how I dodged your best attempt at hitting me so easily."* Sophie said walking away from me.

I followed her out of the building, and then we walked through the city to the opposite end. Soon we stopped walking at a small field, it was the only thing in the city that I couldn't see from the building we were in before. The field was about fifty feet long and about twenty feet wide, it looked more like an archery training ground than anything else. I didn't understand how anyone could do any real training in this field, but I really wanted to know how she pulled off dodging my attacks so easily.

There were a few villagers at the training grounds,

Ten Thousand Walks

Sophie walked up to one of them and said something. Then she pointed at the targets, I looked over at them wondering why she was pointing to them. I soon realized why as she walked up and stood in front of one of them. Then the villager she was talking to stood behind a stand that was about 5 feet away from the target. He took a bow and arrow off of the stand that was in front of him, pulled the bow back as far as he could, and took aim directly at Sophie's head. Then let go of the arrow.

The sight shocked and horrified me, there in front of me, a villager was shooting an arrow directly at his leader's head. What actually happened shocked me even more. The arrow hit the target dead center of where Sophie's head should be. Sophie was no longer standing up against the target. Instead, she was standing directly in front of the arrow. With a smile on her face waving for me to come over to her.

I was utterly amazed at what just happened, I didn't even see her move she was so fast. One instance she was standing up against the target with an arrow pointed directly at her head. The next instant she was in front of the arrow untouched and unharmed. I didn't even have time to think about what to do when I saw the villager let go of the arrow before it was over. I was still shocked by what had just happened, so shocked in fact that I didn't even move or take my eyes off the area. But Sophie didn't give me a chance to get my thoughts together.

"This is called the Phantom style, it seems as though I am teleporting, but in reality, I am actually moving faster than the eye can track. This is accomplished because I'm pushing every part of my body to an extreme state that allows us to move in an extremely accelerated manner. However, this can only be maintained for about a hundredth of a second, which is enough for us to move out of the way of anything we need to avoid. But it can only be done twice every ten minutes by most of us, but it is extremely useful, even though its usage is limited." Sophie said, standing right next to me. I didn't see when she moved, and I could swear she was still standing by the target even though I knew she was right next to me. I turned to her and could see she was tired, she took a deep breath, leaning up against me so she wouldn't fall over.

"Sorry about that I lost my breath for a second, as I was saying it's extremely useful, though its usage is limited to the individual's strength. I have seen the most skilled users vanish and reappear hundreds of feet away in the blink of an eye. Who knows you may even be able to master the skill better than even the best we have here." She finished talking and held on to me as she took some time to catch her breath.

Ten Thousand Walks

It would be a few weeks before I would be able to do very much physical activity, but I was determined to learn this Phantom style. *"You have to teach me how you do that. I'll do whatever it takes in order to learn. I know I'm not fully healed yet but I'm ready to start learning now, so how do I start."* I asked Sophie as she led me back to the hut I was staying in. She looked over at me, seeming to study my body from head to toe. *"Hmm, I'm not 100 percent sure that you would be able to learn this skill after all your father wasn't able to. Nevertheless, I'll make sure you get a chance to learn, and you can try and see if you can actually master it, though I highly doubt it's possible."* She said. I smiled, I was delighted with her response even if it was very skeptical on her end.

We got back to the hut, and before I could ask her what I would need to do first to start the training, she began to speak. *"Before you go asking me what you're going to have to do in order to learn the Phantom style, I'll tell you this upfront I can't teach you. That requires a master far beyond my skill to teach anyone how to use it. So tomorrow I'll bring the master that taught me, with me when I come to visit you in the morning. Until then I want you to relax and get some rest, after all, you're not even as strong as I was when I was a child getting ready to start my training."* She said smiling at me, giving me a look that made me feel like a weakling.

The next morning, she showed up with her master, he was actually quite tall for his people. Almost four and a half feet tall, with long black hair, and very wide blue eyes. He was actually the first person I had seen with blue eyes in this place. He walked up to me, shook my hand and began to speak. *"You can call me master. Your training will begin in a little while. The first thing we will be working on is your ability to focus. Then from there, we will build your physical strength, stamina, and speed."* He said sharply, with a firm commanding voice.

We left the hut and headed to the outskirts of the city, directly across from the waterfall. I was lost in thought as I looked at the waterfall and began to think about what it would look like glowing. However, I was soon pulled out of that thought, by my new master. *"Here is where you will be training from now on. Don't let its beauty distract you it can be a very dangerous place."* I smiled at him for a second as he looked at me with a scorn on his face. It was as though he didn't even want to look at me must less train me.

"I assume you know how to meditate, so I won't have to teach you how to. Sit facing the waterfall and meditate, you will do that until I think that you're ready to move on." He said with a slight hint of anger hidden in his voice,

Ten Thousand Walks

I could tell at this point that he really didn't want to be around me, but I really didn't care as long as he taught me what I needed to know. I sat with my legs crossed and my hands on my knees. I stared at the waterfall for a few minutes and then close my eyes and cleared my mind completely of all thoughts. This was not exactly an easy task to do, after all, that's happened to me lately, but I managed to do it after a few hours of trying to focus on my breathing.

Day after day, I did the same thing over and over again, meditating then sleeping. I didn't understand the purpose of meditating so often, but I did as I was told. I just wanted to learn how to do what they could do, so I did whatever it took to learn.

As the days passed it became easier and easier to meditate, soon I was able to meditate for the entire day without moving a single muscle. Yet still, my master didn't think it was good enough. And even though I thought it was good enough to move on to the next level I continue to push myself harder and harder, I push myself to the point where I stayed in that state for almost an entire week. At that point, my master had no choice but to allow me to move on after all I could meditate for much longer than even he could now.

"Even though I'm not sure you're ready to move on,

Ten Thousand Walks

you mastered the art of meditating as much as you can. The next part of your training will be physical. First, we will begin by training your body to be as strong as possible. After that, I'll be training you on endurance and stamina so that you can use that strength for long periods of time without weakening." This new training would be tough like nothing I'd ever done before. I figured I would be lifting weights of some kind to increase my strength, then maybe running to increase my stamina. Well, I was right about the running part anyway.

The training started extremely odd, my so-called master handed me a black rock of some sorts, the size of my palm, it wasn't that heavy, maybe ten pounds or so. He looked at me and smiled for the first time, I knew instantly from that smile that something was wrong. He pointed to the waterfall behind me, and as I turned back to look at what he was pointing at, he pushed me. It wasn't just a simple push, it was more like a ram, I went flying back past the edge of the city and about twenty feet over the water. I splashed into the water and was instantly pulled down by the rock in my hand. The rock felt as though it weighed a thousand pounds in the water, I couldn't figure out how it was even possible. It was too heavy for me, I let it go and swam to the surface. As I surfaced, I saw my master pointing back into the water. *"What do you think you're*

*doing, where is the rock I gave you, you better go get it
out of the water. Now hurry up and get it back for me."*
He yelled out to me with a very sinister smile on his face. I
could tell he was enjoying every second of this.

I understood why he was smiling before now, it wasn't
because he was finally happy to train me, it was because
the next part of the training was almost impossible. He sat
on the shore watching me and laughing as I struggled to
get to the bottom of the lake. Hour after hour, I struggle
trying harder and harder to get to the lake bottom. I spent
the entire day and wasn't even able to touch the rock at
the bottom. I knew he was thoroughly enjoying this, I also
knew he expected me to quit by the end of the day. But I
was going to make sure and prove him wrong, and wipe
that sinister smile off his face.

I continued at this day after day, it took me a week,
but I was able to reach the bottom. And after a few weeks,
I was actually able to pick up the rock and bring it back to
the surface. He looked at me with that sinister smile still
across his face. I knew the hardest part of training had
just begun. *"Now it's time for you to start building up your
stamina."* He said as he pointed out a trail that ran around
the entire city. *"Now you run, run as fast as you can and
as long as you can, don't stop, just keep running."* He said
smiling as he walked away.

Ten Thousand Walks

I was going to wipe that smile off his face and surpass my father. I was driven like never before, and I ran as fast as I could for as long as I could, day after day I ran the same trail only stopping to eat and sleep. My body screamed at me to rest, but I continued to run, day in and day out. As the days passed, my stamina increased but still, I wasn't able to run once around the city without stopping to drink water. The days passed by, and I watched as my Master sat on the side on the trail smiling at me enjoying every moment of my struggle. The hours of running made everything I had done before in my life seems like a walk in the park. The 150 years I spent traveling the world looking for my father, the mountains I climbed and the oceans I crossed all seemed like nothing. Just running for hours on end at the fastest pace I could go drained my strength to nothing every day, and by the time I reached my bed, I was already asleep.

Chapter 7: Training Ends

Two months had passed since I started training, and I had been doing the running portion of that training for little over a week now. I was at my limit I didn't even think I would be able to make it through the rest of the week. I pushed harder than I'd ever pushed myself in my entire life. Even though I was pushing harder than ever, but I still didn't believe I'd make it through this part of the training.

I awoke on the tenth day of the running training, ready to accept the fact that I wouldn't be able to finish. Then my master walked into my hut, he no longer had a sinister smile on his face as he had for the past couple of weeks. *"Today we will finally be starting the real training. Everything up until now has been child's play."* He said with a serious expression on his face, it wasn't anger or unhappiness at all it was just completely serious. I had never seen his face that way before, and it made me a little bit worried, but at the same time, I was very excited. Mostly because I didn't want to be running anymore. Also, I really wanted to get to start the training the way it was supposed to be done.

We headed back to the waterfall as we always did, he stared at me for a few minutes. *"Now watch closely, pay* close attention to everything I do." He said, then closed his eyes, took a deep breath and began to speak again. *"First thing you must do is envision what you want to do. Then begin to time everything over a few movements in your mind. Your breath, your heartbeat, and how every muscle must be moved. Then you clear your mind of everything but what you're trying to do, gather every ounce of strength in your entire body. Then you give your muscles every bit of that strength all at once. And finally, you move."* His last words were met with action as he vanished. Then from behind the waterfall, I saw his hand waving at me, and then there he was next to me tapping on my shoulder.

"Now before you try to do that, you must first meditate, then we will find a clear path for you to practice on. You will practice moving along this path with your eyes closed at a normal speed, once you've gotten used to it. You will speed up doing it faster each time until you know every muscle that must move to complete the task. You must know every breath you take and every heartbeat that happens along this path. Once you understand which muscles must be moved, and when they must be moved you will be able to speed that up in your mind and then you will try to do a phantom step." He said to me and then vanished.

Ten Thousand Walks

"To be honest, those were the worst instructions I had ever gotten." I said with a look of confusion.

I meditated for a short time, then found a clear path and walked around it a few times with my eyes open. I close my eyes and carefully walked around it again. I stumbled a few times, but after the tenth time around I was able to do it without making any mistakes or opening my eyes to cheat. Then I started running around it, at first, I went slow, after a few hours and a few hundred times around the path I could see it in my mind. I ran faster and faster, going around faster and with more ease each time.

It was a short path, so it was easy to run around it a few hundred times without getting very tired. I rested for a little while as I gathered all my strength together, then I tried it. It worked in a sense, I moved slightly faster than I was able to while running. However, it was still not nearly fast enough. I was moving at a normal rate, though I was running very quickly.

After a while, I began to think I was doing something wrong, or maybe something was missing altogether. Oh well, I thought to myself, it wasn't the worst part of the training, I was at least able to take my time and rest as much as I needed. I continued like this day after day for two weeks, I did manage to speed up a little bit each day. But after the two weeks, I had reached my limit, I wasn't speeding up anymore, and no matter how hard I tried, I went at the same speed. I was begging to think this was as fast as I would be able to ever go, but I wasn't ready to give up.

I needed to do something else, I needed to do something more. I needed more speed, and I need a lot of it. Even if I were able to double my speed, I wouldn't be able to catch up to them. But at the moment I had no clue what I could do to speed myself up. I had hit a dead-end nothing I did was helping me go any faster, I wasn't even getting tired anymore. I was just repeating the same thing over and over again going no quicker and getting no better.

My master showed up and sat on the side of the field I was training in and watched me for a few minutes. *"Well well well, it looks as though you've gotten as fast as you can at this point."* Said my master, I just looked at him and nodded it was obvious that I couldn't go any faster. He just gestured for me to follow him. We got on a small boat and went across the lake to the very edge of where the light from the waterfall reached. He showed me to a cave that looked as though it was carved into the very wall's centuries ago. *"Here on the walls of this cave are the writings that you will need to get to the level you want to be. It holds the secrets to the Phantom style. Once you understand what's written here, you will have the* knowledge you need to learn in order to use the Phantom style properly. After that, you must get back to the village without getting a drop of water on you." He pointed back to the village across the vast expanse of water.

"Oh yeah, you're going to have to bring back one of those fruits too."

He pointed up above me at a tree about fifty feet high with small orange fruits on it. He smiled and then vanished back to the village. I looked up at the tree and could see that everything around it was smooth, almost as if it was polished. There would be no way I could climb up and pick anything without falling back into the lake below. That meant that the only way I would be able to pick any of the fruits would be if I were to use the Phantom style to get to the fruits and pick one.

I walked into the cave, my eyes adjusted to the low light, I soon began to see what was there, and it was amazing. Around me were glowing words, on the walls, floor, and ceiling, but as I took a closer look, I could see that there were three distinct languages. One on the roof and one on the two sides of the cave. However, the floor was something I didn't understand, it looks like a language and numbers at the same time, but they weren't any kind of symbols I had seen before. I stood in awe and shock as a realization hit me.

Ten Thousand Walks

I had been training for this moment my entire life, each of the languages on the walls were ones that I had learned to speak as a child. I never expected to ever use them in my life seeing that no one I had ever met had even heard of them before. The odd thing was I had learned hundreds of languages in my childhood, but there were only a few of them that I had ever used with anyone else but my father. And each of the ones written on the walls was one of those that I had never used before.

I started to read the words on the wall, hoping that not only would it teach me how to use the Phantom style better, but also hoping it would give me new insight into my father plans. However, as I read it, I just became more confused. At first, I thought it was because I was reading it out of order. But no matter what order I read it in or where I started, it was still all total nonsense. It seemed as though it was all just words randomly jumbled together on the walls. Maybe there is a code in here somewhere, I thought to myself as I looked around. After all, whoever wrote this went through the trouble of writing it in three different languages so it wouldn't be that much of a stretch to put it in code also.

Day after day, I swam to the cave and studied the walls. I would spend the entire day studying the walls every single word and every carving of each word. Weeks

Ten Thousand Walks

went by, and before I knew it, I had memorized every letter, every shape and every curve on those walls, and yet I had no idea what any of it meant.

Chapter 8: The Code Of The Phantom

I slowly grew more frustrated, as the days turned into weeks and the weeks turned into months. The words floated through my head every day, I knew them well enough to recite them forwards, backwards and in any order I wanted. Yet still I had no clue what any of it meant, and that fact was driving me insane. I was on the verge of giving up when I had the brilliant idea of translating all three of the langue on the walls and roof into one language. I just knew it was going to work, so I did it, and precisely as I thought it was still complete nonsense. No matter what language I translated them into it always said the same exact thing. Nothing! I just wanted to snap, bang my head into the walls of the cave, until all the words were knocked right out of my head, and just give up.

I had to take a break before I lost my mind completely, I swam back to the city and just sat in my hut for a few hours thinking about the words but doing my best not to. I got up and just ran out of the hut and heading to the path I ran so many times. I sat on the trail until the sun came up and the cave lit up. I stood to my feet to get ready to head back to continue my trying to figure out what the writings meant. I ran off on the path as fast as I could in the other direction of the cave trying to run from the words. I ran faster and faster as fast as I could. Soon the light of day vanished, and I realized I had been running all day, I looked to the ceiling. A wave of blue sparkles ran across the ceiling, my head hit the ground, and I was out, I knew I needed to take some time out from trying to figure things out the instant my eyes opened, and the pain from hitting my head in the fall shot through my body like a bolt of lightning.

After taking a few days off to clear my mind and not think about the code at all, I had a good idea for once. I couldn't believe I hadn't seen it before, the language they spoke in the village was different from any of the ones on the cave walls. But what made this so special was that this language was spoken differently than it was written. I started rewriting the words on the walls, and at first, it seemed as though it was still making no sense at all, but I still had hope, because the way the words in the language was spoken was so much different than it was written.

It took me almost the entire day, but I actually did it, now all that was left for me to do was to read it aloud. I started to read it aloud, but it didn't make much sense making me almost gave up. However, I didn't for one reason and one reason only it was actually making some sort of sense, well more than it was making before anyway.

A Legend Is Born

Ten Thousand Walks

Which meant I was going in the right direction, but I was
still missing one key thing. I went back to the cave sat
on the floor looking up and all around me at the glowing
words wondering what I had missed. The Hours passed by
slowly, my head fell in frustration, and there between my
folded legs was quite literally the key to the whole code.

My legs were covering parts of the letters that were
on the ground, and the part that was left for me to actually
see was in the shape of a key. Then it hit me, the letters
on the ground weren't gibberish or a distraction like I
had thought this whole time. Instead, they were the key
to solving the code. I quickly jumped up, and instead
of looking at the ground as another language, that was
translated badly, I just looked at the shapes and the way
they pointed, and suddenly it started to make sense. The
shapes on the ground where the key to translating the
code, and once I understood that it was only a matter of
time before I could read the code.

*"The code of the Phantom for those that wish to have
the power of the unseen."* That first line put a massive
smile on my face, so interesting and mysterious it sent
chills down my spine. Before it told me anything useful
about using the Phantom style, it started to describe a
fighting style known as the Phantom 10. This was a style
that was used for defensive and not for offense. However,

what made this style so powerful, was because it was a style for fighting off up to ten opponents at once. Not just keeping your opponents a bay, but to take the upper hand from them completely. Thought this was a powerful style to fight off enemies in a one on one battle the true power of this style came when fighting ten. The Phantom style also called the army of ten, was the most powerful fighting style passed down from the world my father destroyed.

Soon after, it began to describe how to properly use the Phantom style, in step-by-step instructions. Now that I had the instructions, nothing was going to stop me from mastering this technique. I began to study it day after day and started to see exactly where I was going wrong before. And exactly how I would master the style. The first and most important step was to get my mind in the correct place, to see the actions I wanted to do and where I wanted to go before I attempted to make them. However, not just seeing them, but also feeling the actions, and become them. Then I had to get my body to a state where it could move faster, much faster than anything I or anyone could normally do. To get into this state required incredible concentration, knowing precisely what is going to be done and where I needed to go. The more I read, the more discouraged I grew. It seemed as though this task would be impossible for me to learn in a few months. It would take half a lifetime to learn everything the code had to teach me about the style to perform it correctly.

However, I'd had it with waiting, and I decided that I was going to do it in under a month. The years of meditation and preparation that was needed to master this style would just have to wait. I was going to do it whether or not anyone thought I could, even if the instruction said it was impossible for me to do. And to do that, I would have to take on this final task in a completely new light than anything I'd ever done in my life. My eyes closed as I pushed the thoughts of failure out of my head, there was no more room for any of those thoughts it was time.

I memorized every word of the code in the exact order it was in, taking it to heart. Following every word of it to the letter. It was working well at first. Though I was moving a lot faster than I had before, I was still not at the point where I would become unseen. So, it was time I took it to the next level, the style required me to be focused beyond anything I would normally do, or have ever done for that matter. I needed to focus more than I ever had in my life. I tried everything I knew to try, but it wasn't enough, I had to do something extreme. Something that could have severe consequences if I failed, I put myself into a deep state of meditation, deeper than I had ever been in my entire life. I was determined to get to the point needed even if it meant letting my body fall apart, if I were truly immortal, I would live if I wasn't, then this would be the last thing I would do.

My mind left my body as it drifted away, I separated every thought, then I separated everything in myself from everything I was focusing on so that only what I needed to achieve was left. My mind let go of the control of my body completely. My mind drifted deeper within itself as the hours blended into days. My heart slowed almost stopping the deeper I got, my breath slowed as the days rolled by slowly. By the end of the first week, my heart and breathing had all but stopped. My mind was lost, and the difficult part began. I was now at the point of no return if I continued and I wasn't immortal I would die. This last thought ran through my mind as I pushed myself forward. As the minute's ticked by I felt as though they lasted for hours, and the days turned into months. My breathing and heart stopped completely for hours on end, my body died and brought itself back to life over and over again, as my mind escaped to find the answers I needed to finally master the style.

As my eyes opened at the end of the second week, I understood everything about the fighting style, I understood how to push my body past the limit's nature had set for it. I stood to my feet, looked around me closed my eyes, focused on my body, and in an instant, I knew everything around me, how far everything was from me, and exactly where the fruit on that tree was. The expressions dropped from my face, and I vanished in the blink of an eye, then I was back standing in the same place with the fruit in my hand. I smiled for a moment, took a deep breath vanishing once again.

I walked over to my master at the training grounds and handed him the fruit, he looked at me from head to toe to see if I had a drop of water on me. Then he smiled even though he still looked annoyed with me. Then I smiled at him and looked at the targets in front of us. *"Fire an arrow at 10 of them at the same time, doesn't matter which ones it is. And I bet none of them will hit their target."* I said with a smirk on my face, he quickly called ten men over to help him and instructed them to take aim. They all took aim at different targets, then looked over at me and then they release their arrows.

The arrows ripped through the air heading straight for each of their targets, I didn't flinch keeping my eyes on every single arrow. Then the instant the first one was about to hit I moved. I vanished. I appeared in front of some of the arrows next to some and behind some of them all at the same time. Stopping every one of them before they had a chance to impact the target, then I let go of the arrows and reappear next to my master. His draw dropped no one had ever mastered the Army of ten before. And he couldn't believe that the first person he had ever seen using it was me.

An outsider.

Chapter 9: The Escape

Ten Thousand Walks

That night I slept with a feeling of accomplishment,
I had achieved everything I needed to in order to finally
escape this place. I awoke, and I knew everything was
going to be different, my body was different my mind
was changed. I was going to use this completely new
perspective on everything to escape this place and finally
get back to my journey of seeing the entire world. I headed
over to the waterfall, I had already picked the fruit, but
a part of me still wanted to do something. Not really to
prove anything to anyone, but just something for me. I
looked into the waterfall as the rushing water fell into
the lake. It was different this time I could see the droplets
moving so slowly. Almost as if time was moving in slow
motion for me, they hit the surface of the water and
exploded outward, and upward. Sending ripples through
the water as smaller droplets flew upward.

I looked up at the tree, even though I had picked fruit
from it already, I didn't know what it tasted like after all
I just gave it to my master. I smiled and put my hand to
my mouth and bit into the fruit, it tasted different than I
expected, like an apple and a banana at the same time a
very strange taste yet still a good taste. I spent the rest of
the day walking around the village taking it easy for once
and enjoying the company of the people. I hoped that I
would be leaving very soon, maybe before the day was

over.

The time for my escape was finally at hand, I was filled with excitement and anticipation. Sophie walked into the cabin that I was staying in. I looked up at her as I packed my things getting ready to leave. *"I guess the day is finally here, it's been really nice having you around these past few months... I kind of don't want you to go."* She started to say to me, I smiled and looked up at her as I stopped packing up. *"But I knew it had to end at some time."* She paused for a little while sitting down in a chair and looking at me. *"They are only two ways you can choose to use to get out of here. The first and most likely the easiest way for you to get to the surface would be to use the way you came in and go back up the waterfall. The second, the way is the way that your father always uses, and that would be to go through the outlet at the very bottom of the lake. So, you're going to have to decide which way you want to take so that we can prepare you properly."* She finished what she was saying, then leaned forward and started to help me pack up.

I sat down and I thought about it for a while, after the training I had been through I knew I would be able to go up the waterfall with no problem at all. However, at the same time I wanted to experience new things, and a very large part of me wanted to know what my father did and follow in his footsteps. With that in mind going back the way I came didn't exactly go along with either of the things I wanted to do. I smiled at Sophie then I answered her. *"I think I'll be going through the outlet at the bottom of the lake, so anything I need to do in order to be ready for it, just tell me and I'll do it."* I said standing up smiling from ear to ear. I was ready to see the sunrise once again.

She smiled at me giving me a hug, then walking out of the hut. *"I'll go inform my master so he can get ready this should be relatively fun for us as well."* She said as she walked out of the hut. I spent a few minutes collecting things that I wanted to keep from around the room to remember this place. I had a journal that I had gotten when I came to this place. But more importantly, I had written the code down and would be taking that with me so I could continue to study it, my goal was to understand it perfectly and learn to use it better than anyone ever had. I had a feeling that the code had more to it than just the army of ten locked in it. I also had to find a way to keep those two things dry in open water, a simple enough task, though it would take some time to actually find what I needed to do it.

After about an hour I was finally ready to get going. I stood at the edge of the village looking down into the crystal-clear waters, smiling with anticipation, I was

Ten Thousand Walks

looking forward to finally seeing the outside world again. I imagined the rays of the sun shining down on me, hitting my skin slowly warming me as I continued along with my journey.

I leaped from the edge of the village, I hit the chilly waters sinking down into it then surfacing a few seconds later. All around me were the strongest men in the village, they would be taking me to the bottom of the lake and showing me where I was to be setting off from once at the bottom. I was ready to begin, two of them carried with them a large board, and the other two took hold of me. I took a deep breath and nodded to them that I was ready. They held tightly to my arms, then they moved, the two with the board moved first vanishing from the water in front of me leaving a hole that I couldn't see the end to in the water that collapsed on itself. I looked over at the two holding on to me, and I was instantly at the bottom of the lake in front of a dark fifty-foot-wide entrance. It was the outlet from the lake that leads back to the surface. I turned as all four of them secured themselves holding onto large rocks on the ground that seemed to be put there for them to hold. They held the board in the other hand bringing it behind me. It was now my turn to do the work.

I close my eyes, focused on the task at hand, and brought my body up to speed. I opened my eyes and

launched off the board, I moved off into the shadows
of the cave at breakneck speeds. Within two seconds of
launching into the cave, I was already more than half a
mile in, and then I felt myself begin to slow. I had already
made it far enough into the cave for the force of the water
to start carrying me. I slowed at first as I moved at the
same speed of the water. I began to move faster soon as
the water began to pick up speed. I had to be careful as I
rushed through the cave not to hit the walls or any rocks
that were sticking out from it or it would be the end of my
trip. This was not a place I wanted to be stuck for the rest
of time.

About three minutes past and the water was starting
to crushing me, forcing me through the cave as the walls
closed in around me. The huge fifty-foot mouth that I came
in had closed in around me and was now little over six
feet wide, yet all the water was still trying to force its way
through that small space at the same time, and I was stuck
in the middle of it. The water fought with me for space
as it pushed me towards the surface. The pressure from
the water, and holding my breath for so long was getting
too much for me, I couldn't take it anymore. I did my best
to hold on as I saw the light from the surface, but I just
couldn't, and I blacked out right before reaching the exit.

Seconds after I blacked out I reached the surface

Ten Thousand Walks

shooting out of the ground with the water in one of the world's largest geysers. My body came falling back down into the lake below and then drifted to the shores where I laid unconscious for the next few hours.

Chapter 10: The Foragers

I awoke a few hours later on the very edge of a lake, I was a bit dazed, my head was pounding, and I had no clue where I came out or where I was. I looked up to the skies for the first time in so long. The light was a purplish-blue color pushing out from behind the clouds as the sun slowly crept into the horizon. I smiled as the rays hit my face, then I looked around I could see the clouds darkening above my head. I would have to find shelter from the oncoming storm that the clouds told was heading my way.

After leaving the city through a cave filled with crushing water, I was done with being soaked in water for a while. I quickly found a little high ground, wasn't very high just about 20 feet above where I was at the lake, but it was high enough for me to spot a cloud of smoke in the distance. I figured it had to be a village, or at least somewhere I could find shelter for the night.

The cloud of smoke looked as if it was coming from about two miles downwind. Which I estimated should only take a couple of minutes for me to travel at my newfound speed. I took a deep breath and look straightforward, then I was gone, I moved out of the valley where the lake was, in an instant. Then I moved into a forest, jumping

Ten Thousand Walks

from branch to branch moving like the wind across the branches not even leaving an afterimage of myself. After a few minutes I stopped to take a break, I must've gone more than ten miles by now. There is no way it could be much further, I should at least be seeing the buildings by now, if not be able to smell the smoke, I thought to myself. I looked up and appeared on the top of one of the taller trees around me, I need to see how much further I had to go.

There must be something strange going on here, I thought, the smoke looked just as far away as when I first saw it. I turned around and looked around trying to spot the lake that I came out in. Which took me a little while, but I did find it and just as I thought, the lake was a lot further back than two miles I could hardly see it. I figured the fire was merely just a lot larger than I'd thought it was originally, so it must be further than I had assumed. I put it out of my mind and took a little break to relax for a little while before I would get back to moving towards the smoke. I estimated I had a half an hour before the sun would set fully leaving me in total darkness, and maybe ten minutes away from the smoke according to my new estimates. I set out again moving a little bit faster than I had before, and actually maintained it for longer periods of time.

Ten Thousand Walks

This time when I stopped the smoke looked much closer, but still it was very strange, I must've gone seven or eight miles and should have arrived before now. Then I took another look at the cloud of smoke, the cloud didn't get slightly bigger it got huge. It was so big at now that I was standing in its shadow and I had been for quite some time. I was still a ways off, but I knew I wasn't very far off, I could even start to see where the smoke was coming from. I took my final deep breath of my break and headed off right for the smoke.

About a minute later and almost two miles later, I was there, I stopped and looked around at everything around me and was completely shocked. There in front of me was a gigantic machine hovering just above the treetops. I had never seen anything like this in my entire life, not even in my father's many labs. I looked around it, inspecting it to see if I could find anything coming from it down to the forest floor, but as far as I could see, there was nothing. I've quickly ran up one of the trees, then jumped off the tree as high as I could to get a better look from above and figure out just how big it was. I flew high into the sky and then looked down onto this vast platform. A part of me couldn't believe just how gigantic it was, it must have been over ten miles long in every direction, it seemed to just keep going and going. As I fell back towards the forest, I

A Legend Is Born

knew this was a city of some kind, and now I wanted to know who was in it.

I ran up the tree once again, and this time I headed for the city, I was going to find out what kind of people lived on it. I flew from the tree through the air and grabbed onto the edge, I pull myself up as much as I could. I reached a small ledge and stood up to a wall the completely surrounded the city. I looked around looking for a way in and soon found it in the form of the small house. As I walked up to it, out came a strangely dressed man, he was about seven feet tall, and he looked as if he was wearing a fully armored suit. I could see that the suit was different from anything I had ever seen, it looks like one solid piece of metal bent around his entire body to fit him like a glove. However, he was walking and moving with such ease that it just didn't seem possible, I couldn't believe that it was metal it had to be something else, I would soon find out.

He approached me and began to speak with a deep boom of a voice. *"Hello visitor, my name is Adam I am the gatekeeper to Forge city, where we make any weapon, any shield, and anything else you can think of for the right price of course."* He said with a smile and then bowed to greet me. I was caught a bit off guard, not just by him bowing, but I had almost forgotten what langue was spoken on the surface. He then turned and gestured for me to follow him back to the small building that he came out of. He walked into the small building and opened the window in front of me, then pulled out a writing pad and some paper and started writing something on it. I was about to ask what he was writing down, but he looked up at me with a smile and began to speak. *"I'm going to need your name, and what you would like us to build for you. Then I'm going to need what you have to trade with us, we accept almost anything of value, whatever you have, we are willing to trade it for our services."* He smiled and looked at me waiting for an answer ready to write everything I said down. *"Well to be perfectly honest with you, I'm not here to have anything built. I was actually just looking for a place to spend the night, out of the oncoming storm. Is there any way that would be possible?"* I responded to him with a hopeful smile.

He looked at me baffled but still smiling. *"Well..., yes, that is possible though it would be the first time anyone has asked to stay here, well since I've been working here anyway. Let me see what you have to trade. Also, any skills that you may have that are unique to you, or you may think is useful in the village are also acceptable seeing that you will be staying here instead of getting something built."* He said, writing something down on the pad, then looking up at me waiting for me to do something or say something.

Ten Thousand Walks

I didn't have much of anything with me except for a few things that I brought with me from the underground city, I had planned on working and earning some money to buy supplies. But looking at the city, I didn't think there was anything I could do to earn money here. Nevertheless, I would try, maybe my newfound skills could be of use here. I looked over at him as he waited eagerly for me to show him what I could do. *"I'm not exactly sure if this skill would be useful here, but I will show it to you anyway. Now keep your eyes on me and don't blink."* I pulled one of the orange fruits I had picked in the city out of my pocket, then took a deep breath as he stared at the fruit. I exhaled, and as I did, I vanished, leaving the fruit floated in the air.

Ten Thousand Walks

Act V

Chapter 11: The Builders

A Legend Is Born

Ten Thousand Walks

The expression on his face was one of pure skepticism, I reappeared and caught the fruit just before it hit the ground. I watched as his face changed from skepticism to excitement. *"Wow, that's some trick. Yes, you can definitely stay the night and for as long as you want in fact. Just answer me one question, how far can you actually go with that little flash trick of yours?"* He asked very excitedly. *"Well to be perfectly honest with you I'm not actually sure, I mean I can go a couple miles at a time, but it usually takes me about a minute before I have to stop to catch my breath and take some time before I can start moving again. But the fact is I haven't actually been able to use this for very long, so it's too early to tell what my limits are."* He looked at me just continuing to smile and jotting things down on his little notepad. Then he got up, opened the door, and gestured for me to come inside. *"Come on, follow me, I will show you to where you will be spending the night, but if you decide to stay with us, we will have someplace more permanent for you to stay."* As I followed behind him, he began to tell me about the city, and what they did in it.

We were walking down a hall as he talked which I thought was somewhat strange, but I assumed this was the wall that I had saw from the outside. Then we walked out into the open, and I was stunned, the city was massive, the buildings stretched into the skies. Reaching into the skies almost as if they're trying to grab the skies and pulled it down, the sides of the buildings shown with glass that reflected the skies as they soared up into it, making it hard to tell where the buildings ended and the skies began.

I pulled my mind back to focusing on what Adam was saying, he was telling me about what the city was and what they did in it. Turns out the reason the city was so large and the reason the buildings soared so high was that the city was a giant forgery. They quite literally made everything one can think of, from the strongest, lightest and safest armor, to the most powerful weapons, they made it all. They didn't just make weapons and shields though, all around me were displays of all the amazing things they made. I seemed to be walking through some kind of showroom, and it was amazing, they made carriages that were more beautiful than anything I had ever seen and lighter than I thought possible. Everything you could ever dream of putting in your house, there was even a small house on display, everything around me was just amazing, I could hardly comprehend how anyone could even build all these things.

As I looked at Adam, the armor he was wearing kept grabbing my attention. It was so sleek bending perfectly with his body as he moved, leaving nothing exposed and unshielded. *"So, I'm guessing that armor that you're wearing right now is what your city is truly known for right?"* I asked him as I walked, he turned and looked at me and smiled looking down at his armor. *"Oh, this old thing, there is no way my city would be known for something as simple as this. Yes, we do make amazing shields, and armor that are even more amazing, but most of our income comes from the weapons we make. We make the only unbreakable swords that can cut through anything right here. Not only can our swords cut through quite literally anything on this planet, but they also do it with more ease than anything else does. Most of the time they don't even offer resistance when slicing through any object."* This, of course, sounded too amazing to be true, there is no possible way any blade could be that sharp. He saw the disbelief in my eyes. Reaching down to his side, he pulled a blade out.

"This is an air blade, named for the fact that when using it, it cuts through almost anything as if it were just moving through the air." He handed me the blade, I took it carefully by the hilt, it felt different from any knife I had held before, heavy but very light at the same time. I spun it around in my hand, and it slipped. It cut the side of my hand like it was nothing falling to the ground, landing and going straight into the ground all the way to the hilt. I was

convinced. The knife was sharper than anything I had ever seen before. Adam picked it up and quickly put it back in its holster, then turned to me with a smile.

"Here we have a very unique saying, with any weapon of great power greater skill is required to use it, or that weapon will turn on its user." I could see why that saying was so popular here; the blade was so sharp that an unskilled swordsman could easily lose fingers, even an arm just trying to remove it from its holster. And someone who had never handled a sword before could easily lose their life just trying to draw the sword.

Though I was amazed by the city and very happy to be in it and getting such an amazing tour of it, I couldn't help but wonder what kind of job I could get here, not being able to make anything at all. *"Now I know that you're wondering what it is that we could possibly need from you that we can't build ourselves. Well, it's not so much about what we want from you, but it's more along the lines of what we want you to help us do. We want you to help us deliver our weapons and shields, and anything else we have to our clients."* Adam said very excitedly, this, of course, confused me greatly, I wondered why a city like this would need anyone to deliver anything, after all, it was flying and continually moving, from what I could tell.

I looked around as he walked and could see many

things that resemble vehicles or at least I thought they
were. *"Yes, as you can see they are many vehicles here,
and they are very fast, but it's still a very dangerous job.
So, having someone with your particular skill set would
come in very handy."* He continued as he waved his hand
at all the vehicles, my eyes followed his hands Looking
around this place, I could see why. If I understood this
place correctly, which I knew I did the delivery boys would
quite often deliver weapons, shields, and new technology
that could turn the tides of war. Meaning they would be
the target of attacks from bandits or the opposite side on
every delivery. They would most likely be getting attacked
by everyone, no matter where they went or what they
were carrying.

I couldn't help but smile, this would be the perfect
way for me to travel a considerable distance with little
effort. It would even give me the time and reason to
practice the phantom style. *"You have got yourself a deal
I'll do it and stay here for a while."* I said with a smile
on my face trying to hide the excitement I felt. I put my
hand out to shake Adams hand as my thought ran off, the
prospect of becoming a delivery boy, was an odd one but
it would be amazing to meet all these new people. Though
it wouldn't be safe in the least, it would give me a good
excuse to get more practice using the Phantom style.

Ten Thousand Walks

I still had to admit, I never expected my first ever job to be so unsafe, I also didn't expect it was going to be something this exciting.

Chapter 12: The Job Begins

My first delivery came the very next morning. The item I would be delivering was a shield, a large one, but very lightweight for its size, come to think of it, it was lightweight for any shield. It was at this point that I noticed something very strange about the city. The city was moving in the opposite direction of the delivery. At first, I thought it was just me, but as I looked at all the deliveries that were set for that day, I realized that they were all in the opposite direction we were heading. This is actually quite ingenious, the way the foragers do business meant that the city was always heading away from where the deliveries were to be made.

The Forge city would move forward at all times, slowing almost to a stop only for a few hours at any one time. They would come to this almost stop just outside of the cities that wanted something made for them. They would make a deal with the city or a person in the city for an item to be made while keeping the city far enough away for it to look like a nearby city. Once a deal was made, and payment was arranged the city would resume full speed as the item was created. It would take anywhere from a few hours to a few days to complete the items that were requested, depending on the item and how many were required. Because of this, by the time the item was completed the city was no longer nearby and the item would have to be delivered, to the person who wanted it, that's where the delivery boys came in.

Seeing that it was my first day on the job, I was only given four deliveries to do by the end of the day. The four boxes I would be delivering that day were loaded into a flying machine that they called a carrier. Which looked very similar to a bird it had colorful wings and everything, but it had a strange opening in the back of it where a bird's tail would usually be, the opening had heat and a small amount of fire coming from it. I didn't pay it any mind, seeing that my mind was currently stuck on how I was going to control this thing. Adam walked up as I was wondering what to do next. *"Don't worry, you won't be flying it, it will be running completely on autopilot. Most of these require someone to pilot them but seeing that you have no clue how to fly one, we figured it was best to give you the one with the autopilot in it. Once you're in it, the system will take over and fly you to the destination, well just above it really. It will circle around for about a minute before it turns back and heads to the next destination point. One more thing, the system is not well fully functional, so after that minute it will go back to max*

speed so better be ready." Adam explained to me, as he
pointed to straps I would be using to strap myself in with.

It seemed easy enough, my job was just to make sure
the package arrived at the delivery point unharmed. The
carrier would fly over the delivery point, then it would
drop the package and me, it would slow down to make a
circle as it descended high enough for me to get back onto
it. What I had to do seemed fairly easy when I thought
about it, I would simply have to catch the package, so it
didn't hit the ground. I would take it to the person and
get them to accept it, then back to sitting in the carrier.
Seemed like I was about to spend my whole day doing a
bunch of sitting. At least the other delivery guys could fly
their carrier and would not just sit and wait all day.

I climbed into the machine wondering how it would
fly, the wings were too small for it to stay in the air. I sat
down in the seat and strapped myself in looking to see if
the wings were going to get bigger. I looked back as they
all cleared away, then the hole at the back of the machine
ignited with fire like I had never seen before. I was pushed
back into the seat instantly being glued to it. It took off
flying faster than anything I had ever ridden in before, and
then it flew higher and higher into the skies. It wasn't long
before I couldn't see the city below me, and I began to get
very cold as the clouds around me fell below the carrier.

Ten Thousand Walks

After which I started to have trouble breathing, I tried relaxing as waited, the carrier rushed through the air, and I soon began to enjoy the ride watching the clouds and the land below me roll by.

The carrier slowed about ten minutes later, and a red light began to flash in front of me, it was time I got to work. I looked over the side of the carrier and saw the package fall from the carrier. I took a deep breath and off I went, within a few seconds I was standing on the ground below looking up. The package was still a ways off falling, I could see it, it was a small dot getting bigger as it hurled towards me. I estimated it would be about thirty seconds before it would get to the ground. I quickly looked around and found where I would be delivering the package, then appeared outside the door knocking. The seconds felt like hours as I waited for an answer, I was so nervous to meet the first person I would be delivering a package to that the excitement was making me crazy.

I was shocked by who answered the door. It was a little old lady, I got the clipboard they gave me to identify the receipts and flipped through it to the page with her name, and there it was an image of her next to the name. I smiled and handed her the pad. *"I need you to put your mark here, and I will collect the payment that was agreed upon."* She placed her mark and head to get the payment and just in time too. I looked back and could see the package was about to slam into the ground. I vanished catching it just before it hit the ground, then I actually walked back to the door getting there just as she got back with the payment. *"Thank you dear, you have a nice day and don't you work too hard now."* She said with a very nice voice as she smiled, I smiled back at her and then turned around seeing the carrier just above the tree lines speeding up and starting to climb back into the skies.

"Well, at least it looks much easier to get into at that height, it was nice of..." My thought was stopped when I realized it was speeding away from me and I had to get on it now. I waved at the old lady then vanished reappearing on a tree next to the carrier. Again, I disappeared and was in my seat just as it went to full speed. I didn't even have time to strap in before being glued to the seat, well not like I need to right now anyway, I can't even move.

As it pulled up high into the skies, I thought this was going to be a fun day. By the third delivery, I was starting to get the hang of it. Turns out once the delivery was confirmed the carrier would finish its circle and begin its climb, speeding up for a few seconds as it set its course to the next point. Then it would go to full power and speed off into the sky at max speed. The trick to not having to push myself to catch up to the carrier was to do the confirmation last. That way I would have enough time to prepare myself before the carrier was speeding off into the sky.

I enjoyed my work for the next few days, making deliveries of all kinds, all over the world. It was amazing seeing the wonders of the world from above, meeting so many different people every day, but the best part was the practicing pushing myself to new speeds. I even got quite good at my deliveries, always delivering everything perfectly every day.

Soon I was approached by Adam. *"How are you doing today Daniel, I have a question for you from my superiors."* I looked at him quite surprised, I really didn't know he had any superiors or who they could even be for that matter after all the only person that ever told me what to do was Adam. *"I'm doing pretty good, I didn't know you had superiors but what did you want to ask me?"* I said to him with a laugh. *"Well, so far you have been doing regular deliveries, which mean no, weapons, large shields, or advanced technology. The reason for this is that these deliveries would not put you at high risk of being attacked. We like to make sure you had got the hang of things before we gave you any dangerous deliveries. But now that you've gotten the hang of things and it seems as though you're the fastest delivery boy we have ever had, we want to give you some weapons, and advanced technology deliveries, but it will be completely up to you whether or not you do it.*" Adam explained to me with a hopeful tone.

I thought for a second about how dangerous it would be, but then I realized that soon I would have to be leaving this place to continue my journey. With that thought in my mind, I figured being exposed to some danger for a while would allow me to practice protecting myself instead of just working on my speed. *"Yes, I'll do it, just tell me what I'm going to be dropping off."* I replied to Adam with a smile. *"Great, I am delighted to hear that you are willing to do this. It will greatly help out the city to have another carrier to do the more dangerous deliveries. I almost forgot to tell you, delivering weapons pay's ten times as much as you are being paid now."* Adam said with a smile as he walked away from me.

That night I got some rest as I prepared for what was to come the next day. I wanted to make sure I was fully rested and ready for anything that could come my way. My excitement grew as I closed my eyes, the anticipation of meeting some many people that were much more interesting than the ordinary people I had met so far, combined with the danger that I might face was just overwhelming.

The morning came a lot quicker than I expected, I had

Ten Thousand Walks

stayed up for more of the night than I thought I would because of how excited I was. But I did get some rest, so I was ready to go, I walked out of the room I was staying in and headed to the area where the carriers were kept. As I approached where mine was usually held, I noticed it was gone. I looked all around and didn't see it anywhere, I knew it was here last night, so someone had to have moved it. I didn't worry too much about it I, just headed to look for Adam he would know exactly where they put my carrier.

Chapter 13: The Real Job Begins

It didn't take me very long to find Adam. It turns out
he was actually looking for me too. *"There you are. I know
you probably noticed by now that your carrier is not in its
usual place. Well, that's for a very good reason, which is
that you no longer have that one instead you will be using
one built especially for you from now on."* He said to me
pointing to the edge of the city, gestured for me to follow
him and began walking. We arrived at the edge of the city
where most of the vehicles were stored when not in use.
"That over there will be your new carrier." Adam said to
me pointing towards what looked like a giant arrowhead.
I didn't think it was a carrier at first look, it didn't look
like it could fly it didn't even have wings like the others.
*"That thing is my carrier, can it even fly, I mean it doesn't
even look like it would stay in the air for more than a few
seconds before it started falling straight to the ground."* I
said as I looked it over with disbelief.

A short man walked up to me as I was talking. He had
a look on his face of annoyed anger as if he was offended
by what I had just said. *"How dare you talk about my
baby like that! I went through the trouble of building this
especially for you. I mean everything will fit you perfectly*

like a glove. But nooo!! The first thing you say is it's going to fall out of the sky. Some people are just so ungrateful, I can't stand them." The man said as he shook his head back and forth, and then walked towards the carrier.

"That's your mechanic, he built the carrier especially for you, and it is better than any other carrier that we have." Adam said to me as he pushed me along to follow the mechanic. *"Well, go on, introduce yourself to him and try to make up for that blunder you just made."* Said Adam to me as he laughed and push me forward faster. I stumbled a little and then started to walk to the new carrier. *"Hey, my name is Daniel, sorry about what I said, but I just don't see how this thing can fly."* The mechanic simply looked up at me shaking his head from side to side scornfully. *"Of course you don't, this is my baby, it's built differently from every other carrier. It's not meant to go slow like the rest, I built this baby for speed and speed alone."* He replied to me in an annoyed but extremely proud manner.

I looked at him. I was very confused, I didn't quite understand what he meant, after all, I thought the carrier I had before was very fast. *"But how in the world would it fly when it doesn't even have wings?"* I asked him confused. He looked up at me smiling slightly then started to laugh. *"Look carefully, it has wings, they are just very small. When*

Ten Thousand Walks

I was building this carrier, I realized that the other ones had a slight problem when it came to going faster. And that problem was drag, their wingspan and their bulky body slowed them down considerably. So, I got rid of it all and started over. This design is made specially to reduce air resistance and allow it to go as fast as possible. That's also why your cockpit has a cover, unlike all the other ones." He explained, taking great pride in his work, pointing out every curve and detail.

I understood what he meant by reducing the drag to allow it to go faster in a way, but I still didn't get how I would stay in the air in this thing. *"Okay, you know best anyway, what's your name."* I said to him watching the packages I was to deliver that day get loaded inside of it. *"You don't need to know my name all you need to know is that I'm the mechanic, your mechanic and the best mechanic there is."* He snapped back at me with a cocky smile and pointed at the cockpit of the carrier. It was about time for me to get going I had a lot more deliveries today than usual.

I climbed into the cockpit, sat in the chair, and then pulled two straps that crossed into an X over my chest. I gave the thumbs-up that I was strapped in and ready to go. My mechanic walked up to the side of the carrier he smiled at me then he began to speak while pointing at things on the cockpit dashboard. *"First of all, this does not function anything like what you're used to. I will tell you everything you need to know so that you don't die out there today."* Die today, I thought what kind of carrier is this. *"First off, you need to know how to get this thing going. That's what this green switch is for, you will switch it into the up position to activate the main engine. Once you switch it down the engine will be deactivated, but because I built this with two engines, switching off the main engine will only slow it down. The second thing you need to know is this button, this blue button once pushed retracts the ceiling of the cockpit so that you can get in and out. Now those are the only two things you actually need to touch in this cockpit. But you need to know one more thing, the systems autopilot can only turn off the main engine, it doesn't turn it on, I made it this way just in case something happens, and you need extra time to get in, or you just needed extra time for something else. Just remember how many deliveries you have, and make sure you manage your time properly, and things will be just fine."* He pushed the blue button and step back, as the cockpit above me started to close.

"Oh yeah, one more thing. It rolls." He said just as the cockpit roof closed and sealed itself. It rolls? What on earth could that possibly mean? Oh well, I don't have time

A Legend Is Born

to worry about that now.

I put everything else out of my mind except for all the deliveries I needed to do that day. I had twenty-five deliveries to make before the day ended. And seeing that I would only be flying around for about twelve hours, it meant that this was going to be a Fairley hectic day.

"Okay, let's see he said switch this switch up to turn on the main engine. So, I'm guessing there waiting for me to switch on the switch to turn on the engines." I was starting to get back into the habit of talking to myself for some reason. I looked around and saw that they had all cleared back, which means they must be ready for me to actually turn the switch on. I sat back comfortably and flipped the switch.

Well, apparently, they weren't waiting for me to switch on the switch. They were actually waiting for the okay from control for me to get going. However, I was jumping the gun quite a bit. So much so that I had started my take off in the middle of someone else's take off. The carrier instantly jerked as the main engines came online, pinning me to the seat as it shot across the launch bay. Heading straight for the edge of the city, in the path of the other carrier that was taking off. I realize what was going on too late, I was heading right for the other carrier and had no idea what to do, I began to brace myself for the crash. But luckily, I looked out the window at my mechanic who was making the oddest gesture pulling something down. I didn't really know what he meant, but I saw a lever in front of me and decided that it was the closest thing that I could pull on and pulled it towards me.

Turns out that's what he was gesturing for me to do, as I pulled the lever as far back as I could the front of the carrier lifted up off the ground and headed straight up. It flew much faster than all the other carriers did, and I didn't feel any shaking like the others during takeoff. I let the lever go, and the autopilot took over leveling off the carrier and increases in speed by almost ten times what the others did. Within minutes, I had completely lost track of where the city was, the carrier was going too fast and climbing even faster, too much for me to be able to keep track of where I was, or where I was going. *"Hey, it's not cold in here, and I can actually breathe well enough to be able to talk."* I said in an excited tone. Once again talking to myself like it was a completely normal thing to do.

Just as I was starting to enjoy the ride, the red light began to flash. *"Aww, just when I was starting to like this ride, oh well, I have to work."* I looked over the side and saw the package fall, I quickly switched off the main engine switch and push the blue button. What happened next caught me completely off guard.

Ten Thousand Walks

The straps that were holding me in place in the seat detached themselves pulling into the back of the seat, then the carrier literally rolled over as the window above me opened just in time for me to fall right out of the carrier. *"AHHHH! I did not see this coming. What am I supposed to do now I can't use the Phantom style in midair didn't anyone tell him that?"* I looked above me, and the carrier was no longer above me, I looked behind me, and there it was. It was looping around, and now it was heading straight for me. Seems as though he actually realized that I needed something to jump off of, but I really didn't want to be jumping off that thing hurling right for me. But I had to, I took a breath, focus my mind, and got ready to begin my job.

The carrier approached me at a high-speed, I turned my back to it then as it came in contact with me I was ready. I moved off of it, flying down passing the package and within seconds landed on the ground looking straight up at the package to calculate how much time I would have left before it would hit the ground. I quickly pulled my notebook out found the recipient's name and image. This time I wouldn't be going to a house, but actually looking for the recipient in the middle of the nearby city, which from the looks of it was quite a cowered city.

This delivery was going to be quite a difficult one, I

estimated about forty-five seconds before the package would be on the ground. I didn't have to find the person that it was being delivered to in that time, but I had to come close. I had landed about two hundred and fifty feet outside of the main entrance to the city. I vanished, off I went to find the largest meeting point in the city. This took me roughly thirty seconds to do. It really helps that I can move at incredibly undeliverable speeds, not that I'm bragging about it or anything.

Once I found the biggest possible meeting place close to the center of the town, I headed back to where the package was to be landing. I arrived just in time, and caught the package within inches of it hitting the ground, I grabbed it out of the air, and off I went again vanishing with the package back to the city. I appeared on one of the taller buildings in the city, which was fairly close to the meeting area. I scanned the area looking for anyone that looked like the guy I was delivering the package to, but it was somewhat hard to tell from the image that I had without getting up close to everyone. *"I can't spend very much longer looking for this guy. I'll guess I leave the package on top of this rooftop and try to get a closer look at the people in the town maybe I'll be able to find him quicker that way."* I said to myself, I put the package down.

I vanished and reappear throughout the crowd of

people, going completely unnoticed. After almost five minutes of looking which to me seemed like hours, I found someone that looked like the recipient. I approached him walking a bit slow as not to scare him, and got a better look at him before I said anything. *"Hello, my name is Daniel."* I showed him the pad with the Forgers mark on it to make sure he was the right person. *"Hello Daniel, I'm so happy you guys are finally delivering my package today, I have been waiting a lifetime it seems."* He put his mark on the pad, then handed me his payment. *"Wait right here, I'll be right back with the package, make sure you don't move."* I said to him then vanished. I grabbed the package and headed back to him, reappearing just in front of him with the package in my hand. His jaw dropped down to the floor as he looked at me then all around to see if anyone else saw what I just did.

I handed the package to him bowed. *"Thank thank thank you. How did..."* I disappeared in the middle of his sentence, I didn't have time for questions I had to get back to the carrier right now. I had spent more time than I wanted looking for him and I really didn't want to mess up on my first important day of deliveries.

Chapter 14: Protect The Package

The sun was in the middle of the sky, and my day was going pretty well at this point, I had already delivered twenty of my twenty-five packages, and I hadn't had one incident at all, not even a broken or crushed package. I laid back in my carrier as it flew through the sky, I decided not to turn on the main engine as of yet I really needed a break, and I was pretty far ahead of schedule, so I had time to take one. Also, from what I had learned of the way this machine functioned these lights meant the next delivery point should be very close by, so not using the main engine wouldn't really add that much time to my delivery time. It would just give me a chance to rest and not be glued to my seat, which was what I needed more than anything else at the moment. I had been going at it nonstop all day, and it was only just past midday.

The twenty-first delivery point would be coming up soon, and though it was short lived, I did get a bit of rest. The red light flashed, and I got ready for the fall, I had learned that unbuckling the belts before the carrier flipped allowed me to have a much smoother fall from it. Which In turn made it much easier to get myself in position to use the carrier as a catapult.

Ten Thousand Walks

The package fell, and I was soon following after it. I landed on the ground, and before I could even look up, I knew something was wrong. It was dead quiet, and I didn't see a city anywhere nearby, I looked at the notepad to find out what the recipient looked like and it just made things worst. *"What? Wait, where's the image what's this."* The pad reads. **"No recipient mark needed payment will be attached to a large tree, collect the payment, and leave the package."** *"Really, have you guys head of the word setup, I mean really, come on guys gees!"* I yelled out into the air.

I looked around the field where I had landed and saw a bag hanging from a tree nearby, that must be the payment, or maybe it's bate. I looked around the area again to see if I saw anyone, then I took a step towards the tree. Whoosh! An arrow flew right by my head. *"I knew it!"* It was a trap I turned, and there was a whole group of angry looking figures standing at the tree line behind me. I sighed and held my hands out catching the package and setting it on the ground in front of me. *"You know you should work on being stealthy, well actually if I were you, I would work on not talking to myself so loudly."* Came the voice of what seemed to be the leader echoing across the field to me. *"Well, I didn't think that there was anyone here to hear me, or maybe I wanted to draw you out and get this over with."* I said in reply as I walked up to the bag and pulled it from the tree.

I held the bag in my hand by its neck, holding it up for them to see. *"Now before we go any further tell me whether or not the payment is in this bag."* I shook the bag and walk back towards the package. *"Ha ha, that's just filled with rocks."* One of the lackeys replied as the leader pulling a bag from his pocket and holding it up for me to see. *"You mean this payment. Now, why would I give it to you when I can just have my men take that package from you. You must not be very smart if you believe that there was really money in that bag."* I smiled, then switch the two bags, pushing my speed as fast as it would go so I would be back standing next to the package before my phantom image faded.

"I would like to thank you for cooperating with me today. Also, for providing your payment and placing it where it was to be kept as promised." I said with a smile as I pushed the package across the field towards them. The leader looked at me in confusion, and just as I was about to take off, he realized something was wrong. He opened the bag in his hand and saw the rocks. *"You switched them. What is this, some kind of magic trick? However good of a trick that was I still can't let you leave with that money. Get him men, kill him if he won't give it up!"* He

screamed, then he turned the bag over dropping the rocks to the ground. *"See I knew thanking you would be too nice I should have just taken the money and left you the package."* I said shaking my head, watching them come straight for me.

By the time I finished finish talking they were arrows coming at me, I knew this wasn't going to end well for me. What made it worst was earlier when I had to move so fast that I would be back before my phantom disappeared, was the first time I had done that over such a large area, and it had completely worn me out. I could still fight them off, but not with the phantom style, which would prove to be a problem for me sooner than later and when I say sooner I mean right now. I dropped to the ground and rolled back and forth barely avoiding the arrows, then without warning one lucky arrow caught my shoulder. *"Oh come on, I wasn't even fighting you, that really hurts you know. I give up already just stop shouting at me already gees, arrows really hurt."* I screamed out as I tried to get to my feet, then pulled the arrow out, which hurt a lot more than I expected it to.

I stumbled to the leader of the group handing him back the bag with the money in it. Well, I may not have much energy, but I did have enough to give them a hard time until my carrier circled back around to get me. I fell forward onto the leader holding onto his clothes. *"Please please show some mercy and spare my life, good sir. Please find it in your heart to let a lowly delivery boy go without harming him anymore. Please please sir, I'm just trying to feed my wife and two baby girls please find mercy in your heart for their sake, so they don't have to grow up without a father."* I said crying, sobbing and pulling at the leader's clothes.

"Get off me you piece of trash, how dare you put your disgusting hands on me." He replied to me as he grabbed the bag back from me and kicked me to the floor. I needed to stall them for about five more minutes to get back enough strength to run. Then I would have enough strength to take what I needed and then get out of here. My plan to do this was very simple; I would grab the bag that was filled with the money then I would just vanish.

The pad I carried had a small button on it that would signal my carrier to return for me, once it was pushed it would take about a minute and a half for the carrier to be above me. Which means I just had to stall them for about three minutes. Then I would push the button, and do whatever I could to avoid using the Phantom style until the carrier was above my head. But that in itself seemed like a nearly impossible task, their leader already wanted to kill me so I had no clue what I would be able to do in order to keep them from just killing me and leaving right now.

Well, there was only one thing I could do, and that was taking something they wanted, which was either the money or the package. Seeing that he was currently holding the money in his hand, I figured I would take the package. I pulled myself up on his jacket again, but this time when he went to kick me away, I moved launching forward at the package. I grabbed it and rolling with it to my feet, then I started to run as fast as I could well really it was as fast as a normal person would run. They came running after me, trying to hit me with arrows and whatever else they had in their hands. *"You fools what are you doing. He has the package in his hands if you keep this up you're going to damage it."* I heard their leader yelling from behind me.

The arrow stopped zooming by my head soon after, then I did something I probably shouldn't have. I turned to see how far away they were from me and realizing they were a lot closer than I expected, I tried to run a little bit faster without actually looking where I was going so I could just focus on running, and not using up too much of my energy.

Just like everything else that seems like a dumb idea at the moment you think of doing it, it turned out to be a dumb idea seconds later as I tripped and fell to the ground

Ten Thousand Walks

with the package in my hand. *"Seriously, what is wrong with me, did I really just trip over my own feet, seriously how did that even happen."* I said to myself as I flipped over to get back to my feet.

By the time I was ready to run again, they had caught up to me and soon after surrounded me. At this point, I had nowhere to go. Running was no longer a choice I had. It was time I stood and fought to protect the package. *"Okay. Let's be civilized, shall we? I don't want to get into a messy, bloody battle, and I'm sure none of you do either. I mean, come on, nobody wants to get hurt today right."* I said with an optimistic smile, holding the package in my hand. I was still hoping they would let me go with the package, or give me the money for it and let me go. Either way, I just wanted to get out of this place and avoid a fight. I really didn't want to die today on my first day actually delivering serious packages. Well, not so much die, but I didn't want to lose a package or any limbs today.

"Well, you are right about one thing we don't want to get hurt. But you're wrong about the battle we do want to fight you." Their leader said with a smirk on his face. I knew things were going to go badly when their leader drew a sword from his side, and they all follow doing the same. Now, it was at this point that I realized my severe disadvantage. I had no weapons whatsoever. Though if

Ten Thousand Walks

I had one, I couldn't use it very well, I had some training as a child on how to use a sword, but I didn't pay it much attention, not to mention that was over a century ago. I looked around as they slowly walked towards me with their swords drawn. Then realized something, the package I was carrying was probably holding a weapon or shield of some kind.

I dropped the box on the ground and punched the top breaking it open. In it was a small circle. I quickly grabbed it and pulled it out to see what exactly it was. On the back, it had a handle just like a shield handle. I grabbed the handle and looked at the front, it looked just like a shield but much smaller. It was a shield though I didn't really get what it could shield being the size of my fist. However, it was all I had and I was going to use it, I held it in my hand and ran straight for the leader. In my mind, I was thinking it may not be a very big shield, but it would be large enough to block a sword. Maybe that's why it's this size, perhaps it's only intended to block a sword while you're fighting, it would make it much easier to move around being this size over a normal sized shield. It would make more sense a large shield in a sword fight most of the time ends up being a disadvantage to the person with the shield. They are always so heavy and bulky, and they block your vision while blocking attacks so you can't see any follow-up attacks or even have a counterattack of your own.

I may not have a sword to attack with, but I'm sure that the shield would hurt if I punch them in the face with it. I ran up to the leader, he swung his sword at me, and this was when it got interesting. His sword came down and impacted the shield, the shield absorbs the entire blow as it pushed closer to my hand. Then something I didn't expect happened the shield extended in an instant it went from being just a little bigger than the palm of my hand to a full-size shield covering most of my body. I quickly pushed back with the shield, sending him flying, and then the shield did something else I didn't expect, it retracted back to its original size.

"Oh, now I can work with this." I said smiling. Even though I didn't quite understand how the shield worked, I knew every time it was hit it extended, and once they were pushed off, it retracted back. After about two minutes of fighting with it, I started to understand how it actually worked. The back of the shield where I held it had a small latch that I could push down to extend the shield, and once it was released, the shield would retract. Learning this little fact made fighting much more natural, now I would swing my fist straight for them and extend the shield at the last possible second, allowing me to hit them full force with the full front of the fully extended shield.

120   *A Legend Is Born*

Ten Thousand Walks

Something that couldn't be done with a regular shield because of how heavy it would be to swing, and how much air resistance it would have while swinging it.

I was able to keep them at bay for a few minutes, even though I couldn't use any of the Phantom style. Turns out that I can't actually fight without it, which I'm assuming would be a problem from how today is going. Especially seeing that I still had four more packages deliver.

I got the leader in my sights, and I launched at him. Extending the shield at the last second and pinning him to the ground. I could hear my carrier coming closer and closer, all I had to do now was get the payment off him and get away from him. I looked up, and my carrier was just insight coming towards me, I released the button on the back of the shield. It retracted and as it did I let it go, grabbing the bag with the payment off his waist. The shield spun around and flipped into the air, and before he could do anything, I was gone with the payment in hand.

I dropped back inside of the carrier sighing in pain, my hand was covered in the blood from my shoulder all the way down to my fingertips. I pulled one of the straps off and wrapped it around my shoulder to stop the bleeding. I sat looking at the switch for the main engines, I reach for it and then stopped. I really needed to rest now, before I would be able to do the next delivery. My hand dropped back down, and I laid back, I was going to leave the main engines off for now.

Luckily, the last four deliveries were just regular packages, and they also weren't that far apart from each other, so I didn't actually have to turn the main engines on until I finished that last one. I switched it on and passed out right after as the autopilot took over and the force from being pinned to the seats knocked me out.

When I finally got back to the city, I was barely able to get out of the carrier. Everyone ran to me to see what was wrong, I climbed out of the carrier and fell to the ground. *"I really hate you guys."* I said then I passed back out before I could even finish getting out of the carrier.

Chapter 15: The shields

Ten Thousand Walks

I woke up two days later in a hospital bed, my wounds were treated with medicine and bandaged up. I looked around the room, everything was white and clean to the point where some of the stuff was so shiny they were almost glowing. I had never been in the room like this before, except for with my father, but he said places like this no longer existed. Then again, I shouldn't be surprised, seeing that many of the things in the city were not supposed to exist according to my father. I was assuming it was not because he thought it no longer existed, but because it wasn't supposed to exist anymore. It was at then that I realized that the city was a leftover remnant of times past. That must be why they are able to build such advanced technology so easily, and so quickly.

I sat up in the bed and began to think, everything around me reminded me so much of my father's laboratories. I couldn't help but wonder if he had come here at some point in time. Maybe he even had something to do with the design of the city, which would be quite interesting if he did have something to do with this city. Knock knock came from the door as Adam pushed it to the side then he walked in. *"Hey Daniel how you are doing today, I hope you're doing good. It seems as though you are doing better seeing that you are awake now."* He said with a smile pulling up a chair and sitting down. *"I'm* feeling a lot better. Just sitting here admiring the design of the city, it's quite interesting." I replied to him while looking through the window.

"Oh, I see, well it is a pretty nice view if I do say so myself." Said Adam to me as he looked out of the window with me. "You wouldn't happen to know who the designer of this city was now would you? It's just that something about it seems so familiar that I was wondering who the designer of the city was." I asked him, thinking about my father and if he had anything to do with this place too, or if I was finally out of his seemingly endless shadow. I hoped that I was going to get the answer that I wanted to get from him.

"I'm not absolutely sure, but I'm pretty sure the person that designed this city was an old guy his name was Carl I think, I'm not really all that sure what his name was, but I know it started with a C. He helped us build the city and get it off the ground almost one hundred generation's ago." He replied to me, giving me the exact answer, I did not want to hear. I knew my father had something to do with this city too, I wondered why he never told me anything about this place too, but right now, I didn't care. This journey was about me not him, and I was going to enjoy myself, even if it seemed like I was just following in his footsteps again.

"So, I'm starting to think that my speed isn't always

going to be enough for me to protect these packages, or
for me to protect myself for that matter. So, I want to know
what we can do to change that." I said to Adam as I turned
from the window, he looked at me with an odd look as
if he had been waiting for me to ask that for the longest
time. *"It's about time you asked about that. I thought it
was strange that you went on all your deliveries without
asking for a shield, or a weapon of some kind before you
left."* He replied to me almost about to laugh. *"I thought it
was kind of funny that you didn't, but I figured you already
had something that you would use to defend yourself,
but after you came back the other day I realized that you
didn't. I thought you had a death wish for a while when
they brought you into the hospital, but no matter how bad
you got or how much blood you lost you just would not die.
You must have God on your side because I have never seen
someone lose as much blood as you did, and still live."* He
continued with a slight laugh in his voice.

    *"Yeah, I know what you mean, but I wouldn't say God
is on my side more like the opposite of that for my family.
But that's a long story I don't want to get into right now.
Anyway, I want to know what I could use to protect myself
from people like those guys."* I said to him then I stood up
and stretched my legs out. *"Well, I will tell you one thing,
you did come to the perfect place to get just what you*

need. How about this, I will arrange a tour of the factories where we make weapons and shields, you can see what we have and pick from those. We will have whatever you pick resized to fit you perfectly. How does that sound?" He said.

That was just what I needed to hear to get my mind off things. *"Sounds great, I'll get myself together to go home, and get cleaned up and ready to pick what I want, thanks a lot."* I left the hospital and headed home to get cleaned up a short time after Adam left. I was very excited about going to go pick out something to use to fight with, but I had no clue what I would be able to use, maybe I could use that shield thing from before that would be good to use. On the other hand, maybe I could use a sword that would be pretty fun. *"I wonder what it would be like to swing a sword when using the phantom style, I don't think anyone would be able to block that or stop it at that speed for that matter."* I said to myself walking out of my house and heading off to meet up with Adam.

I meet up with Adam, he was all smiles ready to take me out on a tour of the whole city. *"Hey Daniel, you're finally here, it's about time too. I've been waiting for you to get here for a while now. Thought you would be a little faster than that, come on, you're supposed to be super-fast, I think you're slowing down from all that sleep you got."* He said with a smirk pushing on my shoulder. *"Oh,*

sorry to keep you waiting I didn't realize you would be
here already." I replied to him. *"Oh no, I was just kidding
around, lighten up I just got here about a minute before
you showed up. Now then, our first stop will be to go check
out where our best shields are made, you might want to
get one of those. After all, I do not think the armor that I
wear can handle moving at the speeds you do."* He said to
me as he walked towards one of the taller buildings of the
city.

"Welcome to the shields building." Came the voice of
a woman when I walked into the building. *"Hello, how are
you."* I replied to her to be nice. She smiled and walked in
front of us, we stopped, and she turned to us. *"My name is
Ariana, and I am the one in charge of this building, I will be
showing you around and if you see something you like I will
be the one that gets it built for you. Please follow me and
I will show you around."* She said, then pushed something
on the wall in front of her, which cause the walls to open in
front of us.

She led us into the room, and as I walked through the
doorway, my jaw almost dropped to the floor. It was just
amazing, all around us were people working on all kinds
of shields, and amour. *"Do you have any idea of what
kind of shield or armor you would like to try and use, or
do you want to see everything we have, I must warn you*

though we have quite a large collection if you want to see them all." Ariana said to me as we walked through the hall surrounded by huge pillars of fire and falling sparks. *"Actually, I do, on my last delivery I was taking a shield that was very lightweight and small that I could extend the size of with a latch on the back."* I answered her as I looked all around, completely fascinated by what I saw.

"I know just what you're talking about, we call that one the Tricksters shield." She said as she led us into a large empty room. *"This is the testing room, here we test how well our shields hold up to other things. I'll have one of the Tricksters brought to you, and you can see how you like using it, if you like it and want one, then we can have one built to fit you."* She said then walked out of the room.

"Is that how you were able to fight off the guys that tried to kill you?" Adam asked. I smiled at him and answered. *"Let's just say you guys should really use tougher cases."* He just laughed as Ariana walked back into the room holding a box with the shield inside of it. *"Here try using this and see how it goes."* She said, handing me the box, then heading to the side of the room and sitting down in a chair that was up against the wall. I looked at Adam as I held the handle of the shield. *"Adam You can fight right? I know I never asked you before, but being one of the cities guards, I always assumed that you could fight*

with no problem." I said to Adam as I moved around to swing the shield from side to side extending and retracting it as I did getting a feel for it as it moved. He looked at me with a smile. *"You know you could just ask me to fight with you to test out the shield."* He answered me as he pulled his sword from his side.

"Move, I dare you." I said to him, and with a smile, he swung at me full force, I quickly ducked, then pulled the shield in place to block his second swing. Swing after swing I blocked, until it was my turn, I retracted the shield and moved. Right behind him, then brought it straight to him, extending it just before it reached him. However, he blocked quickly, I wasn't giving it my all, but I didn't expect him to block it. This time I would get him for sure though, I pulled back vanished and came in full force right at him and as the shield extended he block it again.

"Wow, you're a lot better than I expected you to be." I said, surprised by what was happening. *"Well, I'm not really all that great you are just slow. I mean up until you are about to attack I cannot even see you, but once you start your attack, you move in much slower so I can block you with ease."* He replied to me making me realized what was really happening. It wasn't that I was slowing down my attacks, but it was the shield opening that took all the speed out of the attack. Which, as far as I was concerned

was too big of a downside to risk. If I couldn't fight with my full speed, then I was at a disadvantage no matter what kind of shield I had to protect me.

I walked over to Ariana and handed her the shield. *"This just isn't going to work for me, sorry but it is an amazing shield, thanks for letting me see if I could use it."* I said to her as I handed the shield back to her. She looked at me with a smile. *"You know I don't think you are the kind of person that should be using a shield to begin with. From that little show you just put on for me, it looks as though all a shield would do is slow you down putting you in danger instead of protecting you. Maybe you should try and get something more offensive instead of defensive."* She said to me as she walked with Adam and me out of the room then back to the front of the building.

Chapter 16: The Blades

The next building we went to was not as tall as the first one, but it was still pretty tall, soaring above most of the buildings in the city. We walked into the building, and we were greeted as we walked through the door. *"Welcome to the house of blades, my name is Aden, I am the caretaker of this house."* He said as he walked out in front of us, gesturing for us to follow him while he walked into the next room. I was so expecting the inside had the same layout as in the building of shields.

I was surprised by the more squared look of the inside of the building. Everything was separated into squares, like small rooms, each designed for specific purposes. As we walked through the rooms, I saw many different kinds of blades being made. However, for some reason none of them really called out to me, they were very nicely made knives and blades, but there was nothing I could see myself using. Actually, the fact was I don't think I've ever used any of the blades that I saw here, so in reality, I didn't think any of them would actually work for me. I would most likely end up hurting myself, more than actually hurting the enemy.

Ten Thousand Walks

I looked around at everything and wondered what I wanted to use for my own weapon. Then Aden walked up to me with a few of his best blades. *"These are the best of the best. The sharpest, strongest, and lightest blades we make here. Why don't you take one and try it out, you never know you might like one and decide to use it."* He smiled and headed to the testing room for the building. I walked in and just looked at the box, I didn't really feel like testing out any of them, I didn't even think I want to touch any of them, but I knew I had to try at least one.

"I picked short blades because my wife told me how you fight with speed as your biggest advantage, and that's why you couldn't use a shield, it would slow you down when you fight, and you would most definitely be needing every advantage you can get to deliver some of these packages." Aden said as he opened the glass cover on the box and handed me the longest of the four blades that were in it. I took the blade from his hand, it was not that heavy, but it was heavier than I thought it would be from the look of it. I stepped back and swung it around a few times, then called to Adam.

He smiled, pulled his blade, and lunged at me as if I were his greatest foe, he was ready to take me down for good. I quickly block and contoured him, and then I went in for my attack. Which was blocked just barely, but still with ease. I didn't even try again, I put the blade in the box. *"What's next that one felt a bit too heavy, it threw me off in my attack and made it easy to block even if I was moving faster."* I said to Aden as he handed me another one with a smile. *"Here try this one I think you will find this one much easier to move around with."* He smiled as he stepped back out of the way so that Adam and I could go for it.

I looked down to feel the weight of the blade, it was like it wasn't there, I looked up with a smile, Adam was already in the middle of trying to wipe it off my face with his sword coming at me full force. I had just a second to block. I moved my hand up with the knife and stopped his blade as it came down. One thing happened that I didn't see coming. The knife was too short, and the sword slid right off the side and was coming straight for the exposed part of my arm. I vanished just as his sword would hit me leaving behind a phantom that his sword went through just as I appeared by Aden.

"Yeah, that one will definitely not work, after all, the whole point of this is to have a way to defend myself when I can't phantom step. And if I couldn't move like I just did, I would have lost part of my arm. But I do love how it feels, almost like I'm not holding anything at all in my hands." I said as I took the other blade from him and reappeared

next to Adam. This blade was different from the first two, I thought it was strange that it curved, but I thought why not try it. This time I went in for the first attack. Lunging right at Adam.

He quickly stepped back, pulling his sword in front of him and stopping the blade dead in its tracks. I pulled back, and he pulled his blade up right for me. I swung the knife in my hand and blocked his swing, even though I managed to block it I was thrown back in the process. I landed flat on my back and just laid there. *"Man that hurt, ok I have to say this blade was very nice, but just a bit odd, I just couldn't get the hang of it being curved, it threw me off a bit, what else do you have?"* I asked as I brushed myself off and stood to my feet.

I was handed another curved blade, but this one left me confused it curved backwards. I looked at it, I had never seen anyone use something where the point of the blade was behind the handle next to their elbow. I wondered how this would work I thought. *"What the heck it can't be that bad."* I held it in my hand, and though I couldn't attack with this, Adam was already on his way with his attack before I could even finish what I was thinking.

He came at me, I had no idea how to use this blade to attack, so I dodged backward and punched at him.

Ten Thousand Walks

Landing a blow to his stomach, which I thought, was too easy at normal speed and I realized why it was so easy to land a bow after I saw the blade of his sword coming down for my head, I acted on my first instant. I raised my hand to protect my head, and I heard an unexpected clash of weapons. I had forgotten that the blade was on my arm and it stopped the sword. I smiled this could work as a shield but that's about it, I don't know how I would attack with it.

"That was very unexpected, but at the same time, I wouldn't know how to attack with this blade. So, I don't think you have anything I can use here, which kind of sucks, I don't know what to do about a weapon now." I said as I gave the blade back to Aden. He looked at me then suddenly smiled. *"I know just what you need to do. Before I ran things here, I use to work for someone called the weapon finder. He is known to be able to pick the perfect weapon for anyone, no matter what fighting style they use or how they like the weapons to feel just by watching them move around for a few minutes. If you really want something you can fight with at any moment go to him, he will design you the best weapon possible, then come back when you have the design. My wife and I will build it for you, we haven't had a challenge like you in a while, no one that comes to us ever leaves empty-handed. So, we need to*

Ten Thousand Walks

get you fitted with weapons you can use before we lose our reputation." Aden said as he walked with us back to the front of the building. Then pulled out a piece of paper and jotted something on it and handed it to me with a smile. *"I'll see you soon."*

Chapter 17: The birth Of A Weapon

After leaving the House of Blades, I decided that I would go home and rest up a bit, even though I wasn't tired I knew my wounds needed it and I wanted to be at my best possible state when I went to see this guy. If he was just going to look at me, I didn't want the wound to affect the weapon he designed for me. That night I didn't get a lot of sleep because my mind just kept wandering from place to place, I just kept thinking about all sorts of things. I just wanted my own life I felt controlled by my father still, and I felt as if everything in this city was all just another thing he was controlling in some way. Maybe getting my weapons would make me feel better, after all, my father didn't fight in any way. And if I wanted to get away from him, this would be my first step in doing that.

Though I didn't get much sleep I did manage to rest, and I felt much better in the morning, and I was ready to have my weapon made for me. Adam showed up at my doorsteps to take me to see this weapons master. *"Are you sure you don't want to pick a weapon, I mean really you only looked at four of them and one shield. I'm sure they are tons of weapon's that would suit you just fine if you just go and look at a few more."* Adam said to me as we headed across the city. I didn't know why he was saying this I mean the person we were going to see was recommended to us by one of the people that ran a large part of the production for the city.

We rode across the city in what looked like a cart being pulled along by cables that ran throughout the city. Adam couldn't hold it in anymore. *"He's a whack job ok, there I said it, I know you wanted to know why I do not want to go see him, well that's why."* I burst out laughing, it was the first time I had heard him have an outburst before, but I contained myself. *"Why do you say that I mean he can't be that bad can he?"* I said in response to his outburst, he just looked at me with this blank look on his face for a few minutes.

"He believes in hebedejebe... he doesn't take measurements of any kind and just dismisses everything that's exact and says it should be flexible. But the worst part is he just doodles on everything all the time and mumbles weird things as he is doing it. There is something wrong with his mind. You should go to anyone else to get your weapon built, but not to this guy he will make you something that will get you killed." Adam said in a somber tone of voice, then just looked back to where we were going as if he knew something else that he wasn't saying, something I was better off not knowing, seeing that I

wasn't changing my mind on going.

We arrived at the location that we were to meet this master weapons designer, and there was no one there, which I thought was a bit rude. I didn't know that this guy was never on time. However, that was not the thing that Adam was trying to warn me about, neither was it what he was hiding from me. We waited there most of the day, walking around doing random things for people that kept asking us to help them for some reason. It was like we had a sign on our back that said ask us to help you, we have nothing better to do.

Finally, he showed himself. *"Yooooo what it does yawl. I'm the master, and I'm going to design you the best weapon you have ever used see here. This is my little friend, he helps me out a lot."* He held a pen in his hand as he spoke with a huge smile on his face. Well, huge doesn't quite cover it. It was as if his face wrapped around his smile. And it wasn't a happy smile it was just weird and made me feel as if he was trying to mess with my head. *"Hey, I'm Daniel..."* I was interrupted by him before I could even start talking.

His finger went to my lip, stopping my words and completely creeping me out. *"Shhhh, hush now no words and names are needed just let the universe show us what we need to see."* He looked me in the eyes fixating on me for a full minute in science. *"First off you need to jump on one leg while holding the other with one hand, then touch your nose with the free hand, and you must do this three times, no more no less."* His words came out like a whisper hiding something, I was more creeped out by what just happened than anything in my life, I looked over at Adam. Who was just laughing about to fall over. *"What, I did tell you he was crazy didn't I. Well, what are you waiting for, get to hopping, you are the one that wanted to come and see him, so you have to do what he said if you want his help."* He said doing his best to contain his laughter, even though it wasn't working at all and he was still laughing so much I thought he would choke.

 "Do I really have to do that, I already feel so crazy for just talking to him." I replied to Adam as the weapons designer talked to himself and drew circles on the ground. Then looked up at me and waved. *"Come on you have to hope for me to see the flow of the universe in you, and let the universe show me what it wants you to have. Well, if it wants you to have anything at all, that is. You must do this or risk angering the cosmoses, and we don't want that now do we."* He said not taking his eyes off his circle. I didn't even think he was blinking.

 I didn't want to do anything, but I knew that I had to. I had no choice if I want to get the weapon I needed to protect myself. I stood on one leg and hoped while touching my nose as he watched me with that huge smile and counted. *"One hop yes, this is good, two hops oh yes yes yes, I see I see, three hops yes, I see it now this is it yes it is."*

I didn't know what to do at that point all I could do was just stand as he mumbled weird sounds to himself. *"Yes yes yes, I will do it... I will give him what he needs. Take this paper with you back to the house of knives, and you will have it."* He wrote a few weird shapes and a list of numbers on a piece of paper and handed it to me. I looked down at it, I couldn't figure out what it meant, but I was going to try maybe this whole day was a waste, but maybe not oh well I'll be finding out very soon I hope.

Later that night I headed for the house of knives. Aden was waiting by the door when I arrived. *"You know it's night time right and I sent my workers home a long time ago. But I'm guessing the only reason you're here is because you went and saw him and he gave you something for me didn't he."* Aden said as he walked up to me, I was a bit confused, but I handed him the paper with a hint of hope that when he looked at it, he would be able to make some kind of sense of it and it wouldn't just be the writings of a crazy man to him too. *"Well, what do you think?"* I asked, hoping it meant something to him, but doubting that it did. He looked at it and turned it over and then held it up to the light, then looked at it again. The thoughts in my head went for the worst, it must not mean anything at all.

"Ariana is going to like building this as much as I am, come back here tomorrow at midday, and you will be able to test out your new weapon then." Aden said as he put the paper in his pocket with a grin. He waved to me and headed inside the doors of the building, I wanted to follow him and ask him what was on the paper that I couldn't read that he could, but he closed the door quickly without even giving me a second look. I would have to wait until the next day to find out what he saw that I didn't.

I looked around at the city as the lights slowly went out everywhere except for the house of knives. I was just too excited to sleep at all that night I just wandered around the city, being pulled back into my thoughts of my father and the hand he had in my life. I just wanted his hand out of my life, and I needed to be my own man not the son of a giant. There must be something I could do to walk out of his shadow and into my own light.

I found myself sitting on top of the tallest building in the city looking out across the city, what I saw was the most amazing feat of engineering in the world. The building reached up into the sky all around pulling down the night sky. Crats ran throughout the city from the ground to the tallest buildings, and the most amazing thing was this was all floating along in the sky like it had no weight. This was all thanks to my dad and, I could never make anything this amazing so how was I going to move out of his shadow. The thoughts ran through my mind all night as I sat.

The sun started to rise in front of me, I watched it move up slowly as the city moved away from it slowly. I stood to my feet and turned to look down on the city, what I saw made my heart skip a beat and punch the thoughts that were in my head right out of it. The sunlight hit the buildings, reflected off each other and onto the top of the building in front of me. It made a word, at first, I thought I was seeing things, but then I realized that it said Protect in the language my dad spoke. My jaw dropped as I step forward and my shadow fell over the city. I vanished from the top of the building and headed to my house for a while to try to get some rest before going to see what my new weapon looked like.

I arrived as the sun was at its highest point in the skies and with a smile, I walked up to the door and as I was about to push the door open the doors opened on their own. Aden and Ariana walked out, each holding a case in their hands, smiling away at me. And I knew it, they had made me something I would be able to use, but why were they both holding boxes? I was so confused, then the next person I saw just made it much worse. It was the weapons designer walking out from the side of the building. This was going to be very interesting, I thought to myself.

"The universe said you needed something special. Your road is a long one, and it will be a tough one that you must fight through for longer than we can see. Your father did his best to protect you from your faith, and he has been guiding your steps for a long time, but now it is your turn to make your choice. Either you continue to walk in the path he has set for you, or make your own and walk it." The words that came from the weapons designer was oddly insightful to the point where I was left speechless. He then did something else I didn't expect after the day before. He walked up to me and shook my hand, then handed me a small key and said. *"Thank you, for allowing me to create the designs of my life"* Then he walked away.

I was left stunned for a few minutes. *"Well, that was odd I have never seen him act normal like that in public before. Turns out that whole crazy man thing you saw yesterday is all an act, he does to hide how he does what he does. For him to let you see what he is really like, he must see something in you that is extraordinary. But anyway, this is what he gave you the key to, these two* cases." Aden said to me as he sat the case on the ground and his wife did the same, then they stepped back. I knew what I had to do, I had to become my own man, I had to step into the light and cast my own shadow.

I put the key in the first box that Ariana had placed on the ground, I wanted to know what kind of shield she had made more than anything. I placed the key in the small hole and turned it. The case popped open and inside was something black. I picked it up, it was soft like clothes, it fell open, it was a coat. I pulled the coat over my shoulders, and it fit me perfectly, it wasn't tight, it wasn't too big, and I felt like I could move in it very easily. *"Go ahead, see how fast you can move with it on."* Ariana said with a proud smile. I like the loose fit, but I didn't think it would work when I did a phantom step, my normal clothes were skin tight to keep them from ripping when I moved at that speed. Oh well, here goes, I moved normally first around in a circle then I vanished and reappeared behind them and as they tuned I was gone again back in front of the cases. I could move in it without being restricted or having it ripped apart, this was amazing. *"I made ten pairs of pants with them and two coats. I made them so they would be comfortable, but still be able to move with you. But the most amazing part was they are shields like no other, able to stand up to a lot more than anyone can*

Ten Thousand Walks

really hit you with." She said with a smile.

I couldn't take it anymore, I had to know what was in the next case, I reached down and open it. Inside were two curved blades that were nothing like I had seen when I was in the House of Blades. *"Those are yours they will work just the way you think they will."* Aden said as he pulled a ball from his pocket. I picked up the two knives and held them in my hands they were amazing. Dark black blades all the way up to a ball that was right before the hilt. The hilt fit my hands perfectly and had a small latch at the top. They were both the same length, but I wondered why they were curved the way they were. I held one up to my arm and the blade stretch from my wrist to my elbow. *"Hold them and push the latch at the top it will do exactly what you think."* I held both of them, I swung them a bit they moved like the wind, and I smiled.

I held them in my hand, then I broth the hilts together, pushing the button at the bottom, and it did just what I thought, the blades pulled back on the ball, running along my arm from my wrist to my elbow like a guard for my hands. Then what I really wanted the ends spiked the opposite way of the blades curve. I smiled and turned as he threw the ball, and I vanished, the ball fell on the ground and split into four pieces.

"Adam, let's see how you handle him now." Aden said

A Legend Is Born   **147**

then, I saw Adam walk out of the building with a new sword in his hand. *"I got my sword upgraded let's see if you can handle me now with a lighter sword."* Said Adam with a smile as he ran for me. He brought his sword down I flipped my knives back and blocked it, then I attacked with the other hand. He jumped back, then swung again; I pushed my knives forward as I blocked and Adams sword slid down getting caught at the end of the blade. I pulled up throwing him off balance, then attack with the second blade stopping just before cutting him. *"I gave up I just can't keep up with you now."* He said as he returned his sword to the holster.

"*Those blades are my greatest work, they are able to cut through anything, unbreakable, and they never go dull. The blade atomic structure is designed to heal itself as it cuts to ensure the bald remains the same down to the atom no matter how much it is used."* Adan said as he walked up to me, and picked up the two cases.

"*Wow, these are amazing, I can't believe this I'm so happy, thank you so much."* I said with a smile, I was so excited. As I was about to head back home, Aden waved to me, I turned, and he spoke words I had almost forgotten with a grave smile.

"*With any weapon of great power, greater skill is required."*

148   *A Legend Is Born*

Chapter 18: Shadow

With my new outfit and my knives, I had no trouble defending myself. Lucky thing to seeing that I was now running into trouble on a daily bases, but with my new tools I was leaving every encounter without a scratch on me. Soon I was only given high-class deliveries to do, which for me was great, I got one or two of them each day, and I got paid more to do them than I was when I had ten to fifteen regular ones. This gave me time to do the one thing I came to the city to do, and that was to see the world, I would take time out to look at all the places around the area I was going every time I was out on a delivery. Sometimes I would even spend half the day in one place exploring before going on to the next delivery, or if it was the last one I had for the day. I would just spend the night and return to get my new deliveries the next day. Before I knew it three years had passed, I had seen so much and done so much in that time. I even got a nickname in the city from the other delivery boys. They called me the shadow because all that was seen when I fought was a black shadow attacking my enemies.

Something began to happen in the city that was just off. I couldn't put my finger on what exactly was the problem or what was going on that was strange, but I knew something was going on. Everything in the city felt off like something was going on, but then again, I might have been wrong, after all, I didn't fully understand everything about the city and I didn't know everything about it. However, I had a feeling something was off just by the way Adam was acting now.

A few months after this strange behavior started, I was given a very odd delivery to do. It had no recipients, and no collection of payment all it had was a drop-off point. All that was written was: This package must be set on the ground. Then the delivering person must leave within a twenty count of setting the package down. I thought this was odd and I had to know why the instructions said this.

I took the package to its drop off point, set it down, and then vanished. I fell back out of sight and did the count, once I hit twenty, someone showed up out of nowhere. *"Wait a minute, did he just phantom step?"* I said aloud shocked by what I had just seen. This just couldn't be a phantom step, it must be something else. I had to know what it was now not later. I appeared behind the person, pulled my blade, and then moved it to their neck leaning them back into me so they couldn't run. *"How did you do that, and what is in that box."* I asked as I pull my blade closer to their neck, touching it just a bit.

A Legend Is Born

Ten Thousand Walks

"The same way you did, and if you can move like that, you should know what's in this box." Her voice said calmly. What she said caught me by surprise what could she mean by, I should know what's in the box if I move like her. *"I have never seen anyone use a weapon while moving like this, you must be something special. But I'll tell you what's in the box. I'll even share it with you if you lower the knife."* She said, I was a bit resistant at first, but I lowered it from her neck but not fully. *"Now tell me what's inside of the box I want to know what's in it before I decide to change my mind about lowering my knife."* She slowly turned to me and held the bottom of the box to open it, then the white in her eyes turned blue, and she vanished.

"I was hoping you would make this into a challenge." I said with a smile, then I vanished, reappearing right behind where she had stopped. *"You're cute you know, but come on, you don't expect me to be that easy to get away from when you have one of my packages."* I said to her as I took a step closer to her, she gasped for air. *"Come on, leave me alone, it's not like I didn't pay for this its mine and I need it."* She said as she stumbled over herself a bit then vanished. *"That's so cute she thinks she can get away from me, like a little kid running from a parent."* I said to myself thinking about what she said, and what she meant by she paid for it and she needs it. *"Oh well, I'll be finding out*

Ten Thousand Walks

soon."

I appeared behind her walking to her, she was stumbling as if she was in pain trying to get away from me. *"Lady, are you ok. Well, I know that's a dumb question I can see you're not doing ok. Guess you're feeling the effects of moving so fast aren't you."* I said to her as I walked up to her. She turned to me just for a moment, and I saw her eyes were now blood red, which wasn't a cute look. Then she pushed herself up as much as she could, I knew what she was going to do. I looked up and saw that the valley ahead of us had a steep ditch in it. I knew if she tried, she would end up in that ditch most likely dead. *"Lady don't..."*

She was gone dropping the box as she vanished. Good thing I was much faster than she was. I disappeared just after she did and appeared holding her flying backwards straight for the ditch. I had caught her and took the hit from the rocks in the ditch just in time. Good thing too, because that really hurt and I was wearing a suit of armor. There was no way she would have lived if I didn't catch her seeing that even the clothes she had on were already ripping to pieces from her movements.

"Hey, lady are you ok?" I said as I shook her gently, but she was out cold.

Well, this wasn't very good, I hoped she would be

152   *A Legend Is Born*

ok, but I wonder if she was the only one coming for this package. I cover her up with my coat, and then went back to the drop point to see if there was anyone else coming. I waited there keeping an eye on her until the sunset after it did, I figured that there was no one else coming. I set up a small camp, and carried the woman to it, I thought about taking her to the city, but I realized that it wouldn't be a good idea.

I looked at the box and then snapped it open. Inside was maybe twenty small bottles. I picked one up and inside it was a blue liquid, it was see-through yet it was almost glowing. I had never seen anything like it before, so that meant that it wasn't natural. *"I just don't think it's possible to bottle the phantom style, so it must be something else that was giving her the ability to move that fast."* I said to myself, holding it up to the moonlight. I was in the middle of looking at it when she yanked it out of my hand. She pulled the cap off the bottle and was drinking it before I knew it. *"What is wrong with you lady why would you drink that, God only knows what's in it."* I said to her.

She looked at me, her eyes blue again, then she looked at the box and then back at me. *"You didn't drink any, so I have the advantage now."* She said with a smile, making me laugh. *"Really, you have the advantage I don't think so, you almost killed yourself earlier, and look at your clothes they are all ripped up, even your skin is red and bruised, look at me, I don't even have a scratch on me."* I said to her with a smirk on my face. She looked at me and kept looking back at the bottles. *"You don't know what this is, do you?"* She asked.

"Nope, I don't know what it is, they don't tell me what's in the packages I'm delivering, just where to take it and how much to collect for it." I said answering her. I was hoping that now that she was talking, she would tell me what I wanted to know. But, I didn't think that was going to happen anymore as she pulled the box and cover it, sitting holding it behind her back then just stared at me. I knew she must be in a lot of pain and couldn't run from me anymore even if she wanted to, the pain would shut her body down if she tried again. She must have realized that she didn't have the advantage as she started pushing herself back with her feet trying to protect the box.

"Look, you see the coat that's over you right now? That's mine and its worth a lot more than that package by far trust me. So why don't you just tell me what's in that box." I said to her. *"It's called Shadow. It's a drug that lets you move very fast for very short burst. You must be taking it too, if you were able to keep up with me. So why don't you look like I do, is there a different one that you take that doesn't have these side effects."* She said to me trying to

keep her hands from shaking. *"I'm not taking anything to be able to move like this. I have been training for years to do this, maybe even longer than you have been alive. How old are you anyway?"* I spoke in a very low voice as not to make her feel like I was cornering her.

"I'm not young, I'm almost as old as you are I'll be twenty-five in a few weeks." I burst out laughing, I couldn't hold it in when she said that. *"How old do you think I am?"* I said, trying to contain my laughter. After a bit, I stopped laughing, and she answered me. *"30? I mean you can't be that old."* I was shocked by how old she thought I was but then again, I do look very good for my age. I thought smiling. *"No little one I'm closer to 200 than I am to 25, I'm actually over 200 years old, but I stopped counting. I figured that there was no point in counting if I was never going to die, it just seemed a bit childish and well out of place for someone like me."* I said to her with a smile.

She looked a bit less on edge as she let go of the box and wrapped the coat around herself more. *"So, tell me something, why would you take anything that does this to you?"* I asked her. I just couldn't think of any reason why anyone would willingly take something like that. *"Because it gave me the power to do things that I could never do without it, to fight like no one else, and to keep my family safe. I would gladly die to protect them this pain*

Ten Thousand Walks

I'm in is nothing." That was shocking to hear from her I did not expect her to say that at all. *"Well, I expected you to say something else to be perfectly honest, I expected something much more selfish."* I said to her as the thought dawned on me that the drug was coming from the city.

My mind was now filled, with questions about what was going on in the city, maybe this was why they have been acting so weird around me lately. They were watching me this whole time trying to see how they could copy my powers. *"How much did you pay to get this?"* I asked her, she looked at me, and then backed up a bit. *"I didn't pay for it, I wanted a weapon very badly, but I couldn't pay, and they gave me this. They said if I could use it and show it off they would make me anything I wanted and I did, but now I need it to feel better, to stop the hurting inside."* She said, coughing a little.

Her words confused me and made perfect sense at the same time. Though it was true that they were all about making a profit, they also loved making new things. Getting her to test their latest weapon in exchange for a weapon she wanted would be a simple trade that benefited them more than it did her. And from what I could see from how much pain she was in and how hurt she was, she had the bad half of that deal. *"What kind of drug is this anyway and why would you keep on taking it*

Ten Thousand Walks

after what it's done to you." I asked her, she was quiet for a while, shacking and coughing a bit as she looked around nervously, then she answered. *"It's not my choice once you taste the power you can't stop you need it, or your body hurts. Shadow is like nothing else it changes your whole life with just a taste."*

This thing, Shadow, was far too dangerous to be on the market, my abilities should never be in the hands of a normal human who hadn't spent the time training their body to use it. And it should most defiantly not be in the hands of someone that wants to use it as a weapon. I had to find out who in the city was making this stuff and I had to stop them no matter the cost.

I would be taking her back to the city once she rested and recovered maybe she could help me find the people responsible for making the drug. Then I could stop them and hopefully find a way to get her off needing to take it at the same time.

Ten Thousand Walks

Act VII

Chapter 19: The Break

Ten Thousand Walks

The next morning, I woke up to find she was gone. *"Really lady really, did you really run off in the middle of the night. Geez, she must have a death wish or something, whatever she's lucky I need her help."* I said talking to myself as I got up and stretched for a bit, I looked around to see which way had the best path for her to run along. *"What! Where's my carrier what the, did she steal it from me. Oh, I'm going to make her pay now, you're going to regret this."* I said yelling out in anger.

Little did she know my carrier can only fly back to the city, or maybe that's just what she wanted it to do. Either way, it was headed to the city, and I knew she couldn't have left that long ago, and she wouldn't know how to fly it at full speed so I would be able to catch up to her I think.

Lucky thing I had a compass of sorts, well it didn't point north it pointed to the center of the city, showing me the fastest way back to the city in case I had ever gotten separated from my carrier. Well, it wasn't really all that lucky I had been carrying it around since I started doing the deliveries, it was something I never thought I would need. However, the lucky part was it was in my pants pocket this time and not in my coat, most of my coats had pockets except for two, funny thing the one I had on and the one I was getting pockets put in were the only two without pockets.

Ten Thousand Walks

Now I knew which way the carrier was heading, it was nice that the carrier used the same thing to set its heading back so I could catch up to it if I got left behind. I flipped it open finding the direction I needed to go then I headed off as fast as I could, vanishing and repairing miles apart. Only stopping long enough to correct my path and I was off again within seconds.

It took me some time to catch up to her, and by then I was utterly exhausted. I was on the brink of falling over when I appeared on the carrier. *"Man, I hate it when people run..."* I managed to say before falling inside of the cockpit trying to catch my breath chocking from trying to breathe.

I took a few minutes to just sit and catch my breath, my heart raced and my breathing was heavy. I thought I was a lot better than this by now, but I still needed more practice to be able to move like that for too long. I could feel my heart still beating like crazy as I calmed down, it was a good thing I couldn't die, or I would be right now. Which, come to think of it I didn't fully understand how it was even possible. I mean there had to be some limit to what I could go through and what I couldn't, my life must have an end at some point in time. *"Why are you looking at me like that, you pervert, I'm not meat, and I'm too young for you."* I heard her voice interrupting my thoughts.

Ten Thousand Walks

It was then that I realized that I was gazing at her and I didn't even know her name.

"So, what's your name you little thief, it better be a nice one for you calling me a pervert Missy." I said to her before losing my breath once again. She just looked at me, I could see she was trying to find a way to get away from me, but the expression on her face showed she was stuck. "Fine I'll tell you my name, its Annabella, and I am not a little thief ok I didn't try to steal this thing. It was just cold last night, and I wanted a warm place to sleep, so I got in here, and when I work up, it was in the air and heading somewhere. It's not my fault!" I just looked at her with a smile I was going to laugh, but I was too out of breath to do that. I'm sure my smile didn't help with the whole pervert thing, which for some reason I didn't want her calling me.

"See, you're a pervert stop looking at me like I'm just an object to please you." Annabella yelled as she slapped me. "Look lady, I have a name you know, it's Daniel, and I am not a pervert so stop calling me that would you it's not nice. Anyway, the thing you are in right now is called a carrier, and it took off because you took my coat in it. We are heading back to the Forge city, it's where this thing goes after I finish all my deliveries. Which reminds me, you're going to help me find the people that makes this

Ten Thousand Walks

Shadow thing, and you're going to help me stop them you got that." I said to her trying to sound very serious, which is an extremely hard thing to do when out of breath. I must look like a fool, which I was guessing that's why she just smiled at me. Then she pulled my coat around her tighter and leaned against me closing her eyes.

What on earth is with this lady I thought to myself as I took a few deep breaths. We should be getting to the city in a short while. I could speed up the carrier, but at the moment, I was tired after chasing this lady more than 200 miles. I honestly just wanted to take a nap for the rest of the day. Sadly, I couldn't see that happening any time soon, I had to find a way to hide this crazy lady when I got to the city so that the people making the Shadow wouldn't find out about her and hide.

A few hours passed by far too quickly, I saw the city coming closer it was time to get started now, the carrier would be going in to land in just under two minutes, and I would need to get her out of the carrier and hide her without anyone seeing her. A very overwhelming task but, I had a plan to get her in the city unseen. There were vents that let out the smoke and hot air from the city's engines, and one of them was just under where the carrier would land. The best part was the one that the carriers landed above only let out hot air, and not smoke so that the

A Legend Is Born

carrier polite could still see.

I pushed the button to open the ceiling above me. Annabella opened her eyes to my smile, I wrapped my arms around her and kicked at the stick in front of her sending the carrier into a barrel roll. I moved vanishing from the cockpit with her in my arms and appearing on the ground, then from there inside the large vent hole. *"I need my coat, and for you to wait here for me, I'll be back for you soon ok, and I'll bring you real clothes to."* I said to her then vanished with my coat, I was back in the carrier grabbed the stick and stopped the roll.

I landed and got out, then headed over to get my new assignment, seeing that I was gone the whole night. I expected to have a few, but oddly enough, there weren't any new ones. I didn't mind, though it meant I would have to come up with a reason to come back and get Annabella later, which I already had a plan for anyway. However, it would mean she would need to do something I knew she wouldn't want to do at all. I waited and rested at home for about an hour, then I decided to go and get my plan started.

I watched as the sun was at its highest point in the skies, which meant most of the delivery men would be coming back and heading out at the same time. It was their busiest time of the day. It would make my plan so much easier to do. I headed to the top of one of the nearby buildings that I usually go to when I need to think. Then I descend down from there using a phantom step and heading to the edge of the city. From there I went over the side lunching off of one of the cities stabilizing wings straight to the ground, then to the vent before I could be seen by anyone.

I appeared in front of her with a smile. *"I'm going to need you to jump."* I said to her turning my smile into a serious look I hoped.

She looked at me and laughed. *"You're a funny pervert... I'm not jumping from anything."* She said laughing at me. *"But you have to, don't worry, I will catch you before you fall too far. I'm going to be on the ground, and I will need you to jump when I give you the signal."* I said back to her, the smile was gone as she realized I was serious. She pouted and folded her arms, planting her feet to take a stand. Yep, this is going to be harder than I thought. The words floated through my mind

I headed back to the top of the city, I looked all around, and then I jumped from the city edges. I landed on my feet with ease and looked around, there didn't seem to be anyone watching me at the time, which was good. What I was about to try was just very, well I wouldn't say it was safe, but it passed that at this point, what I wanted to try was just dumb, no if ands or buts about it, it was just a dumb idea. It would be the first time I would ever try to use the phantom style and change directions while using it, without coming to a stop and going again. It was hard even when coming to a complete stop to instantly go in a different direction, but this time I was going to try and run along the bottom of the city and then around the side. I would actually have to make a full turn, which I never did before, and I didn't know if it was possible to change directions that much while moving at that speed.

I took a deep breath and just let all my worries about what I was about to do fade away. I gave her the signal to jump and watch as she just laid back and fell from the huge opening. She fell back with her hands stretched out as if she was about to just turn over and fly away like a bird. I took my last deep breath as she reached the halfway point between the city and the ground. I dropped my head down and focused everything on what I was about to do. Time slowed for me, I opened my eyes for the first time when using a phantom step. The world stood still all around me, I looked up and saw her frozen in the air above me ready to be caught.

I moved with everything I had, my hands wrapped around her pulling her from the air, within an instant my feet made contact with the bottom of the city. My momentum pushed me up against the bottom gluing my feet to the underside of the city. It was the moment of truth, I moved my feet, and my body moved along the bottom of the city. Moments later it was time for the hardest part. I would now have to turn up the building. I moved my feet and pushed the air behind me with my hand in the hopes it would let me turn up the side. It had worked I was flying up the side of the city, but it was getting harder. I had to go from going straight up to going horizontal into the city. I grabbed the edge of the city walls, but it wasn't enough to stop me just change my directions slightly.

I appeared on top of one of the taller buildings close to the edge of the city, stumbling to the edge with her in my hands. I barely made it, but I didn't have time to stop now, I vanished right as I reached the edge of the building, hopefully before anyone saw me. Four rooftops later, I appeared in front of my doorway and went in as quickly as I could. It would have been much easier if I had left the door opened or just cracked so I could walk straight in, but I had locked it out of habit.

I kicked the door shut behind me and put her down, I was a bit tired of carrying her, and she opened her eyes shocked. *"You caught me, you really did, wow am I in your place?"* She said as she sat up and looked around. *"Yes,*

Ten Thousand Walks

I caught you, did you really think I wouldn't. Never mind, don't answer that. I know you didn't think I would. Anyway, that's not the point, it's time you tell me who the person getting you this drug is." I replied to her as I sat down in the chair across from her. Trying my best to seem like I wasn't tired even though I fully knew I was at my limit.

"Before I tell you anything I want to know what you did with the rest of the bottles, and you better not have thrown them away." She demanded, I just laughed and pointed to the package on the table. *"That's all of them well I took one I need to know what's in it in order to know what part of the city it was made in."* I said to her waiting for an answer to my first question.

"Ok, I will point him out to you." She said, looking around my place. *"Anyway, how are you going to find out where this came from, are you one of the scientists here, because I was told that they don't make deliveries."* She said as she walked around going through everything. *"Well, I have been here a while, and I do like to read, I have also been reading everything I could get my hands on while here, it gives me something to do on my devilries. After all, it gets annoying flying around the same places when you have nothing else to do. So, I have been able to learn a lot about how things work, but mostly how they make the medicine they use here. So maybe I can find out how*

it's made, or at least where it's made." I explained to her as she walked into the room I slept in, then looked around and flopped down on my bed. *"I found where I'm sleeping, where are you sleeping tonight, pervert."* She said with a smile snuggling up to my pillow.

"Where you're laying right now, that's my bed Missy. And can you please stop calling me a pervert my name is Daniel, I told you this already." I said to her trying to sound serious and in charge. She just looked up at me. *"Oh, this bed is so soft I'm going to miss sleeping here it sucks we are going to be leaving soon."* What she said, confused me and before I asked anything, she threw a small piece of paper through the air at me. *"He's the one that had the idea to do this. He told me in person where to get the packages and when they would be dropped off. He even told me how long to wait and where to hide so no one would find me out."* She said burying her face in my other pillow, kicking her feet up and down to get her shoes off.

I caught the paper and slowly flipped it over to see the image on it. I was shocked and left speechless when I saw it. It was the leader of the Forger city and Adam. I looked up to her about to ask her who was the one she meant. *"It was the two of them, the tall one I think his name was Adam, he was always with the other one to keep him safe. Adam held the packages for me, and the other one was the* one running everything." My best friend and the leader of the city my father left behind were the ones doing this. My mind filled with disappointment and anger, I understood now what she meant when she said we would be leaving soon.

I looked at her laying there, my mind stuck in thought. *"Get some rest you're going to need it, we leave tomorrow. I am going to need a way to stop this drug, but for now, I don't have the skill needed. However, I do know where we can go to get the skills I need to counter this drug. I'm going to find out where they make it and take as much as I can and destroy the rest of it. Then we will make a break for it, I will need to say goodbye to this city for a while."* I said to her, but it wasn't really for her it was for me.

I vanished from the room, leaving her in bed, I appeared on the tallest building in the city, sitting down. *"I was meant to protect this city wasn't I, how can I protect it now when they are the ones that are doing the things that I try to protect others from."* I said to myself getting lost in my thoughts, trying to figure out what I would do next. All I could think was it was time to move on until I had the strength to do something else besides just destroy a bunch of bottles in a lab.

I sat there until the day blended into the night, I calmed my mind, and waited for an answer to come to me while meditating on what I knew I had to do, but didn't want to bring myself to do. All night I thought until the sun began to stretch its rays over the horizon, it was my last sunrise here, and now it was time to go. I looked down on the city below me, it was still dark, and it would stay that way for about two more minutes. I vanished appearing in my room, she was there waiting on my bed with a bag and my coat in her hand. *"Let's go, we have a lot to see, well we have a lot that you are going to show me."* She said with a smile as she stood to her feet.

I pick up the piece of paper that she threw at me yesterday, and I wrote on the back. *"Thanks for the carrier I think I'll call it a Plan from now on. Oh, before I forget, you should close the lab."*

"Get to the launch area I have something to take care of first." I said to her and vanished with the bag and my coat. She walked out of the building and vanished. I appeared in the lab where the Shadow was made then I went nuts. I let out all of my anger all at once destroying the lab in seconds, then I just picked up my bag, filled it with the small bottles that were left unbroken. Then I vanished, leaving behind only a small fire where I was standing.

"Are you ready to go, it's going to be a very long flight to where we are going." I said to her getting into the plane

Ten Thousand Walks

with her. She looked at me and asked one question. *"Can you move up some pervert I'm still sleepy, and I want to sleep."*

I laughed as I pulled out the auto polite and threw it out of the plane and then hit the launch button, switching the main engines on at the same time.

Chapter 20: The Run

Once we left the city I knew where I needed to go, it was a faraway place that would take a bit of time to get to, even in the plane. I had found out about this place when I was traveling in search of my father many years ago. I wasn't sure what the city was actually called, but I liked to call it the city of healers. Everything they did there was dedicated to healing the body from whatever illness it had, and they had taught me a lot of things about the body. They were also the reason I became so interested in science.

The sun began to set, and I put the plane down in a small field of grass, to set up camp for the night. I looked around the field there wasn't anything around us, just a few trees spread far apart. I couldn't help but think there was nothing that could be used for cover if we needed it. *"We will spend the night here, tomorrow we will be heading out on foot. So make sure you get plenty of rest."* I said to Anabella as I set up a tent for us to sleep in. She looked over at me with a confused look on her face then spoke. *"Why would we go the rest of the way on foot when we have that flying thing to use, wouldn't it be faster if we just flew the rest of the way?"* She asked me as she pulled some of the bags out and sat on them, putting her face in her hands as she pouted. *"Well, it's not about how fast we get there, but more of getting there without trouble, I know they're going to be mad that I took the plane for one and two what I did before leaving must have made them a little toasty."* I explained as I finished setting up the tent.

"That and they can track the plane, so if we travel in it, they will be on our trail by the end of the day tomorrow…" I paused for a moment thinking if they would catch up before then. *"So, in the morning I'm going to send the plane off in the other direction we have to go from here on out. Besides you will enjoy the walk it's not that far from here, I think it should just be a few days hick."* I said with a smile getting into the tent and laying back.

"Are you going to stay out there all night or are you going to come and get some rest." I said and paused for a second as I waved at her. *"Maybe you think I'm going to do something to you, you know I'm not a pervert even though you think so, I'm a really nice person you know."* I said again as I closed my eyes, I didn't care if she came in or not I was still too tired from the day before to think anymore. I didn't sleep the night before, and after chasing her all day yesterday, I was already about to fall asleep while setting up the tent.

The morning came much too quickly for my liking.

Ten Thousand Walks

Before my eyes could open, I felt something on my arm moving slowly. I opened my eyes and looked over at what was there, and I saw her there snuggling up to my arm. *"Awww, you're so cute like a little girl, and I thought you didn't want to be next to me in here."* I said waking her from her sleep.

Slap!

She hit me right across my face a lot harder than I expected her to be able to. *"Shut up you. You pervert it's your fault you had one tent, you just wanted to try and get me in here so you could have your way with me."* She said as she pushed me away, I just laughed and got up. *"Come on pack up your things we have to get going in a bit. There is a lake about a mile up from here, we will stop there and eat before hiking. I will go get rid of the plane while you get ready for the journey."* I said to her as I walked over to the plane and started packing everything up for the upcoming journey.

It didn't take us long to pack everything up and be ready to get going, we hopped into the plane and off it flew. I brought it down by the lake to let her out and to take out what we would need for the journey. Then I headed back in the other direction along the path that we were taking the day before, then changing it slightly so it didn't just backtrack on the same path and get found quickly. I jammed the controls with some rocks from the lake so it would keep going straight. I pushed the button to open the hatch and waited a few seconds to make sure it was not changing directions. Then I push the button to close the hatch, followed by the button for the main engines and vanished from the seat.

"Hmm, I wonder how far they are behind me. I know there's no way that they would just let me leave just like that." I said to myself as I fell to the ground. I landed did a quick looked around me then vanished. I reappeared at the top of a tree a few hundred feet away. *"Did you hear something?"* I asked myself as if I was going to answer back. I looked all around to see what I could have heard. I heard it again, a whispering sound coming from the distance. I turned and looked, and there in the distance were five carriers headed this way. I smiled and vanished.

I went from one phantom step right into another all the way back to the lake. Something I soon learned wasn't a good idea when I wanted to stop. I appeared at the edge of the lake, trying to look like I was totally the man. But, going from one phantom step into another meant I was actually gaining a bit of speed each time, and the air behind me was following me with a little more force with each step. So, instead of coming to a stop next to the lake, I appeared and stumbled, almost falling into the lake.

Ten Thousand Walks

Then, as I tried to play it off the force of the air that was following me, hit me and sent me flying about three feet in the air and falling straight into the water.

"Oh wow, is that how you look cool, I mean I know you're from a different time than me, but was it ever cool to get knocked into a lake by the wind." Anabella said laughing at me. *"Oh, ha ha very funny, I'm glad that I amuse you."* I said back to her as I walked out of the water. *"Did you make us something to eat, I'm hungry."* I asked her as I walked over to the fire that was there. *"Yes. I made food, but not for you I made it because I was hungry. You can have the leftovers."* She replied to me, with an annoyed tone even though she had already taken the food out for both of us and hadn't eaten yet. *"Well, thank you for giving me some of your leftovers."* I said with a smile sitting next to her and eating. She just glanced over at me and eat her breakfast.

After I finished eating and getting ready to go, I looked at her with a very sinister smile. *"I'm going to need one of the vials of shadow. I am also going to need you to actually learn how to use the phantom style the right way, so take one of my coats and put it on, it will protect you some so that you can move a bit easier."* I paused handing her one of my coats and looking around. *"Do you see that tree over there?"* I said, pointing at a tree a few hundred feet away.

Ten Thousand Walks

"Yeah, I see it what about it?" She answered me with a confused tone. *"Well get going you have a minute to get there, I need to see how you actually move before I can help you move the way you should."* I said back to her as I put my backpack on and pulled it tight.

She looked at me angrily, then vanished, I watched closely as she moved to see just what she was doing that was hurting her body. She arrived at the top of the tree, and I smiled then I moved appearing next to her a few seconds later. *"Let's go no time to waste."* I whispered in her ear as my hands went around her waist, I moved vanishing taking her with me.

I kept going pushing myself from one phantom step into another without stopping. Spinning around trees as I moved to rush through the forest, leaving a path of broken trees behind me as the air that followed me ripped through the leaves and branches behind me. I stopped after twenty miles at the top of a tree, then just dropped straight down from it and vanishing again. A few feet from the bottom, appearing on the ground looking up and watching the top of the tree get ripped off by the air that was following me.

"We can take a break here for a bit, I'm going to take a nap can you make me something to eat after all it's only fair I've been carrying you this whole time." I said to her

smiling with my eyes closed, expecting her to slap me. *"Yeah, I'll make you something for when you get up."* She said as I heard her walk away from where I was laying. I was left speechless. There wasn't even any anger in her voice. Maybe she was hungry too, even though we had eaten about a half hour before. On the other hand, perhaps she was actually being nice to me now, and she was over the calling me a pervert thing.

"Wake up pervert you have slept long enough, I made you something to eat even though I shouldn't have." She said as she pushed me, waking me up from my nap. **"I guess not."** Was the first thing I thought as I opened my eyes. *"Yeah yeah, I'm up now let me eat, we have a long way ahead of us for today."* I said as I stretched a bit, then took the food she handed me.

"So, you have a few problems when you move." I said to her as I ate the food she made. *"What you need to do is relax first, it seems as though you are working against yourself when you move because of how tense you are. This taste good by the way..."* I glanced up at her smiling and continued. *"Anyway, what you need to do is to plan your movements before you move, plan all of them so that you are thinking what you will do after your next two moves before you make the first. Also, you need to clear your mind of all other thoughts. It will help you relax and*

Ten Thousand Walks

focus on the task at hand."

I finished eating and stood up, then looked around and spotted a small clearing about half a mile away on the side of the hills where we were about to go into. *"There I want you to get to the clearing right there make sure you do what I told you and you should be able to get there with no problem."* I said with a smile as I pointed at the clearing.

She looked at it for a while then and vanished, I gave her a few seconds, then I pulled the straps on the backpack I was wearing tight, then I disappeared. I showed up, turned around, put my hands out, and caught her, as she appeared falling forward. *"That was a lot better and sees it didn't hurt this time did it."* I said with a smile. *"You still need a lot of work, but we will work on it tomorrow when we arrive."* I wrapped my hands around her. *"Hold on tight, we are going a lot further this time than we did before."* I said with a smirk and vanished.

I stopped to rest for a few minutes every few miles for the rest of the day. However, we spent most of the day moving. Though we could have walked I knew that I should hurry and get there to get her looked at, I had a strange feeling that something was off about her. I also had a good idea that the cause of it was the Shadow, which was actually the reason I was teaching her how to move better. Maybe if she knew how to move better, she wouldn't hurt her body so much and wouldn't need the Shadow.

The sun started to set and I stopped for the day, we had traveled almost four hundred miles already, which finally meant we could walk the rest of the way tomorrow, that and I was exhausted. We set up camp for the night in a large valley that lay at the bottom of a volcano. We could see the smoke rising from the top, but there was no glow which meant it was still inactive

The stars filled the sky uninterrupted by any clouds, the moon was nowhere to be found, and it reminded me of the time I spent in Gods Mouth looking up at the fake starry ceiling. I thought about my life so far, all I had done and how far I had come in such a short time. The wind blew across my face and felt as if it was rocking me to sleep making my thoughts fade away. I closed my eyes, I figured I would sleep out here tonight and let her have the tent all to herself.

I was awoken the next morning by a tug on my arm. It was her getting all comfortable with my arm. *"Really, it's time to wake up we have a long day ahead of us Annabella."* I said to her as I pulled my hand from under her slowly. She just looked at me with a blank expression that screamed, I got caught. She didn't say anything at all as we got ready for the long walk ahead of us. Which I honestly found to be a bit disturbing.

A Legend Is Born

Ten Thousand Walks

We soon headed towards the volcano, it was an easy walk, for now, we were in the flat valley before the base. Once we passed that we would hit the hard part, we would have to climb going up two miles and only half a mile forward so pretty much climbing straight up. *"I think I want to skip this part, hey do you want to carry me for a change."* I said with a straight face, hoping for here to give me her normal reaction, but instead of a slap, I got a look. *"No, you just want to be on top of me you pervert. Don't go thinking I like you because of last night. I only did that because there were bugs in the tent, I think you put them there to scare me."* She said as she looked at me with an angry look. I just laughed it was nice to see her back to her usual self.

We began the very steep and long climb up the side of the volcano, it wasn't long before we were tired and needed a break. As we rested, I looked over the side to see how far we had gotten, and was disappointed that we had barely even gone anywhere. Looks like this climb was going to be a lot more difficult than I had originally expected. *"Do you think we can make it to the top by nightfall?"* I asked Annabella while drinking some water and looking out and up at the top of the volcano. *"No, that's not happening, it just isn't, I mean really, do you see how far up the top is. We will be lucky if we make it there tomorrow."* She replied to me, then stood up and began to climb again.

We climbed until the sunset that day. *"Let's stop I can't keep going I can hardly see. And I'm a girl stop making me work so hard you pervert."* She said as she sat down on a small rock that stuck out from the cliff face we were climbing up. I looked at her and then I looked up, we were only an hours climb from the top, and there was nowhere for us to sleep safely here. *"Sigh we can't stop here, it's not safe, we could fall if we aren't paying attention. I guess I'll have to carry you up the rest of the way. Take the rope and tie it around us then hold on tight, this is going to be a lot bumpier than before."* I said to her as I helped her wrap the rope around us and handed her the end so she could tie it behind me.

I took a look at everything around me then found a good solid rock to stand on to get started from. Then I took a deep breath as I looked to see where I could jump to, then vanish. I went from rock to rock as quickly as I could vanishing right after I appeared on it in order not to stay on them for too long. I wasn't going to take the chance and wait to see if the rock or where ever I appeared would hold our weight. A few minutes later and we were at the mouth of the volcano looking over into it as clouds of white smoke slowly drifted up to us.

Ten Thousand Walks

"We are here finally! The city of the healers is below us are you ready to go." I said to her then jumped into the cloud before she could give me an answer.

Chapter 21: The City Of Healers

Ten Thousand Walks

We flew through the cloud and landed in the center of the city, everyone around us stood still looked over at us then back to what they were doing as if it was nothing out of the ordinary. *"Really, you people must have problems. We just fell from the sky, and we get no attention not even a greeting."* Annabella said as she pulled at the rope the pushed me away and dusted herself off, all while not stopping her mumbling about how perverted I was. *"Oh, stop it you know you liked me carrying you, and you need to relax. To these people you aren't that weird, falling from the sky is how anyone gets here. Though falling without ropes or anything is a bit different."* I said back to her laughing.

I took her hand pulling her behind me as I walked off. *"Come on, it's time for us to find a place to rest."* I said as I pulled her along. *"What do you mean us. You need to find me a place to rest away from you, not together with me, you big pervert trying to get me alone."* She said to me, she said this while holding my hand tighter, but she was still hitting me. Such a weird woman doesn't even know what she wants herself. I thought to myself as I walked.

I took her to the center of the town marked by a tall building. I walked into it and was greeted as I entered the doorway. *"Daniel it is so good to see you again, it has been too long."* The voice of an old woman said from behind a desk across from the door. *"Hello again Miss May, it's been a long time I'm surprised you remember me."* I said back to Miss May walking up to her and hugging her. *"This is Annabella. I'm going to need a room for the two of us if you have one. I'm not sure for how long I will be here for. It might be a few days, but more likely a few months I'm not sure yet."* I said to her while I looked around the inn. Nothing much had changed in the forty years since I was last here. Well, almost nothing, the old woman uses to be a girl just about 10 years old, now it looks as though she is running the inn, her parents built and from the looks of this place, she is doing an excellent job of it too.

My attention was brought back to Miss May as she began to speak again. *"You can have the room you were in the last time. I don't get a lot of people this time of year. You do remember the way to the room right."* She said to me as she walked around Annabella. *"Oh, by the way, do you need a room for her to or is it just the one room."* She said as she walked back to her desk and opened her book. *"No, the one room is good, I'm sure she won't mind one bit."* I said with a smirk, which was quickly followed by a slap. *"The one room is just fine, not like that pervert won't try and come in the other room if there was one anyway."* Annabella said as she took the key to the room and walked off.

Ten Thousand Walks

I just smiled, then I walked in front of her heading to the room, I opened the door as I started to speak. *"Let's get some rest tonight ok, and I will show you around the town in the morning. It's actually a very nice city here I'm sure you will love it."* I said to her standing next to the open door to let her in.

That night was very quiet, I assumed it was because we spent all day climbing that she had no energy to complain about anything. Before I could even try to say something to her, I realized that she was already asleep. So, I let myself out of the room to go out for a bit I needed to find out more about the drug, and I had a good idea who could help me, if he was still there. I headed to the house of one of the healers I knew the last time I was here.

I knocked on the door and waited for someone to come to the door. *"Hey Paul, it is Paul, right?"* I said as the door opened and a tall man stepped into the doorway. *"Yes, it is. Do I know you?"* He said, as he looked me up and down. *"Wait is that you Daniel? Oh, wow, it is you. You haven't changed one bit. I mean wow, how do you do that."* He said jumping to me and hugging me. The last time I had seen him, he was just ten years old, and one of the smartest chemists in the city and I don't mean for his age, he was better at chemistry than any of the adults. I just wonder how much better he had actually gotten since

Ten Thousand Walks

I was last here.

"*Come in, come in, what brings you to see me today my friend.*" Paul said as he showed me inside and to have a seat. "*Well, I need your help with something that's very important to me. Well, actually, it's not just me, it's important because it's a drug that gives people extra strength, but slowly kills them as a side effect. Not just that, but it's very addictive. I want your help looking for something to counter it. I need to get anyone taking it off of it safely.*" I said to him. "*Well, that's something I can and will be more than happy to help you with. Just one question I want to know why you want my help. Why is this important to you?*" He said to me as he leaned forward in the chair he was sitting in. "*Well, it's because the drug gives the person that takes it, an ability that I have spent a very long time learning to do, so it's my fault that it's even something that people can get addicted to. So, I have to fix this.*" I said, answering him.

"*You haven't changed a bit have you, well I will help you. Do you have a sample of the drug with you or a blood sample of someone that has taken it lately?*" He asked me laying back in his chair. I pulled out one of the vials filled with the drug and handed it to him. "*Oh yeah, I wouldn't take any of it if I were you, by the way.*" I said as I stood to my feet about to leave. "*What does this thing do to a person anyway?"* Paul said as he held the vials above his head, looking up into it as it swirled and glowed. *"This?"* I said as his eyes came down to me, I vanished from them, tapping on his shoulder from behind the chair making him jump up. I smiled as he turned then I vanished from the house. Standing just outside the doorway. *"I have to go for now, but I'll be back if you have any more questions."* I said to him, but he was speechless all he did was wave at me.

I headed back to the inn for the night, I was actually really tired, the past few days I have been pushing my limit none stop and not getting very much rest. And even though I couldn't die, I could still pass out like anyone else. Which is what I felt like doing at the moment, I didn't even think I could do another phantom step. Which I wasn't about to try and do anyway, I just wanted to lay down and sleep the day away well, maybe the next few days. Unfortunately, I knew that wasn't going to be happening, so waking up late the following day would have to do for now. Until I got things in order anyway, then I was going to take a few days for myself just to sleep. *"Yes, just a few more days in bed and I'll be all yours for a few days just you and me."* I said as I hit the bed and was gone fast asleep as I finished talking to myself.

The next morning there was a tug at my arm, I felt as if someone was trying to wake me up earlier than I wanted to. So, I did the right thing in my mind. I just ignored it until it stopped. Eventually, I woke up and got out of the bed to find that the room was empty. *"That's odd, I thought she would still be sleeping here too, I didn't think she would leave after I didn't get up this morning. Oh well, I'm not missing out on anything now am I. Man, why do I still talk to myself after all this time, I really need to stop doing this."* I said to myself, then walked to the window, looking out of it to see what was different about the city since the last time I was here. It didn't look as if anything had changed, besides paint on the buildings.

Downstairs, I saw Annabella waiting for me talking to Miss May. *"About time you woke up, your lazy self-up. You promised me a tour of the city, now it's time for you to keep your word, I'm waiting."* She said as I walked up to her. *"Yeah, I know don't rush so much I was coming to find you so we can go anyway, so just take it easy ok."* She looked at me, lifted her hand as if she was going to slap me, then she just put her hand on my cheek and patted it softly. *"Good boy."* She said with a smile, then turn back to Miss May. *"Thank you for everything I will be seeing you tonight someone has to take me out today."* She said to her. *"Well, you have fun now and don't let him get out of line with you ok."* Miss May replied as Annabella stood up and began to head for the front door.

190   *A Legend Is Born*

Ten Thousand Walks

We walked out of the inn, and I pointed to a tower that was close by. *"Up there is where we will start. I have something to show you."* I vanished and reappeared at the top of the tower, she was close behind me. *"What is it you have to show me that we need to be up here for, it better not be something perverted or I will kick you off of here got it."* She said with an annoyed voice. I just laughed for a second, then I pointed out. *"Just look around."* I said to her.

What was around us was what made this city so special of a place. The city wasn't built on top of a volcano, but it was built inside of one, and it was an active one too. At the side of the city, lava could be seen flowing out from under the city. The entire city was designed to keep the volcano from erupting and to keep the people in it safe.

First off, most of the buildings were in the center of the city, which was lower than the sides. This way the weight of the city itself would push the lava to the sides of the city as it came up. The sides of the city had large trenches dug into the ground that would release the pressure from the lava that was being pushed out, by letting some of it run out and off the sides of the hills.

However, the part of this that was most ingenious was the pumps that pumped water up from the bottom of the volcano from a Lake two miles away from the bottom. How it worked was so simple, yet it worked so well. It was lava powered. At the sides of the city where the lava flowed out, it would push against metal panels that blocked the outlets, the force of the lava would move the panels and turn a gigantic pump. However, that pump wouldn't be nearly strong enough to pump water up so high. Therefore, what they did was use a pressure pump that pumped more water the harder it was pushed down. The lava flowed out right on top of the pressure pump and would push it all the way down pulling the water up from the lake. Then, once the pump was driven all the way down the top would lean and pour all the lava out. Which would move the metal panel that directed the lava to the next side of the pump. Allowing the process to start over as the other side pushed down and rest the opposite side.

The water was then pumped into a large pool at the center of the town, which connected to small gutters that run out to help cool the ground in the center of the city and to provide clean water all the buildings in the city at the same time. Which was heated to kill almost anything that could get someone sick. Which was one of the reasons most people here became healers so that when people came here to relax in the healing waters, they could go to the healers in the city for anything that still bothered them. I explained to her as I pointed everything out. *"But won't that water get dirty after a while."* She asked with a confused look on her face while looking into the crystal-clear waters in the pool that sat below us.

I laughed and spoke. *"Aww, I thought you figured it out. The water is pumped in there, then pumped back out to all the homes in the city, then it is pumped off of the sides to cool the lava and help things grow. Also, a lot of it simply boils away in the center of the town, the water there is clean because it's always fresh water coming in and water going out and no used water coming back. Where do you think the cloud, we jumped through came from if the volcano isn't erupting?"* I said to her with a smile. *"Let's go for a walk and take it easy for the next few days we have plenty of time before we need to get started with anything."* I said to her, then took her hand and headed to a door that was behind us.

We spent the next few days just relaxing and wandering around the town. I also took the time to get to know Annabella a bit better. I wanted to know why she took the Shadow in the first place. But I really wanted to know if she was involved in anything else, or if she was being used like she said she was. I couldn't be too careful anymore after this, I needed to be sure I wasn't the cause of anyone else's suffering, and I needed to help her as best I could.

Chapter 22: The Drug

The sun rose high into the sky the next day, and I headed over to see Paul. I wanted to see how much work he had gotten done on the drug. As I walked to his house, I looked up, thinking about how much I loved this place. Maybe it was because I wasn't all that fond of the sun and the town was in the Shadow of the sides of the volcano for most of the day. On the other hand, it could be how the people were always looking for new interesting things to study and learn just like I was.

My mind wandered back to what I was doing as I reached Paul's doorway. *"Hey, Paul you in there? I hope I'm not bugging you too much I just wanted to see if you looked at the sample I gave you yet. I know it's only been a few days, so it's no big deal if you haven't."* I said from outside the door, then waited for an answer. After a few minutes, I figured he must not be home. Oh well, I will come back later. Then, as I walked away from the door, I heard Paul's voice. *"I'm coming, I'm coming don't leave."*

I turned back, and he opened the door to let me in, he was wearing a plastic apron and had a mask on, that was pulled down around his neck. *"I was actually looking at the sample you left me it's amazing. Has it really been days since you left it with me? Feels like I've been looking at it only a few hours."* He said as I walked into the house, I noticed he was wearing the same thing he was the night I came to see him. *"Have you been looking at that since I gave it to you?"* I asked him a little bit shocked but not surprised. He looked at me, smiled and pulled the mask up. *"Well, yes I mean at first I just wanted to see if it was just the bottle or if it drug was actually glowing but then I got carried away. You have no idea how complex this formula is, it's just well amazing."* He said to me from behind the mask as he walked away, he walked through the house and into his lab as I followed him.

There were pieces of paper all over the floor and desks in the room he used as his home lab. *"So, have you found a counter agent to it yet, or have you found out how it works?"* I asked, hoping for a yes, but he just looked at me with a weird smile and then turn back to the microscope as he started to speak. *"Well, no I haven't, well not yet anyway. I have figured out a few things about how it works though. It's amazing to say the least, just amazing. The drug affects every part of a person's body, it enhances their muscles, gives greater focus, even increases the amount of oxygen the body takes into the blood with each breath of air taken... I'm sorry, but honestly, it will take me months to figure out how to make a counter agent that is safe for* someone to take with this. However, I am almost at the point where I can copy the formula and make it a little less powerful." Though it wasn't exactly what I wanted to hear it was better news than I expected to get.

"What do you mean by less powerful anyway, do you mean taking away some of what it can do?" I asked him, wondering how it could be less powerful, I mean it only did one thing really so it must mean he was making it have less of an effect. *"It's simple really, the drug affects the body, and it affects the atoms that your body is made of separately. Seeing that I have figured out how it affects the body, but not anything else I can lessen that part of it."* He answered me, leaving me even more confused than I was before asking the question. He looked up from the microscope to my confused face and then back down again. *"Well, you see the drug is useless unless you can actually focus enough to active it. By lessening the potency of the part of the drug that affects your body functions I can lessen how long a person can actually use it for also I should be able to remove the withdrawal side effects, well that is eventually anyway. Though it will take me about a month to come up with a formula that will have that effect."* He explained to me, this time I understood what he was saying, well I mostly understood.

"Ok well, you can take your time on finding a counter

agent if you can do that. But I have one more favor to ask you." I said as I looked around the room with a big smile on my face. *"Yes, what do you want to ask?"* Paul answered me looking up from the microscope. *"I want you to teach me."* I paused as his face light up some. *"I want to be able to help heal others not just protect them."* I continued, he looked happy but very shocked. *"Well well, what brought this on? You use to be all about exploring and seeing the world, now you want to be a healer and a protector. What's with the whole life change?"* He said as he pulled up a chair eagerly waiting for an answer.

"Well, it's nothing really just that I feel as though I've been running from who I am and after my journey looking for my father and finding him, I'm starting to realize I've been wasting my life. There are so much more important things I could be doing with my life other than just seeing the world." I said to him with a serious look on my face.

"Well then, I'd say it's time we get you started then. The first thing we will be doing to start your training off as a healer will be to start understanding this drug seeing that you have such an interest in it." He said to me while showing me to the telescope. *"Though I can tell you everything in here I can't for the life of me figure out how they came up with this mixture it's just an amazing feat or pure dumb luck, I think."* He continued to talk about what

was in the drug most of which went over my head when he used technical terms, but I did manage to understand how the parts of it affected the person that took it.

The drug functioned in four stages, from what I understood the first stage gets the body ready. At this stage, the drug begins to flow through the person's bloodstream, getting into the organs and cells. Enhancing their normal functionality. The muscles of the body would be lined with the drug strengthening the muscle fibers as it mixed with the natural chemicals given off by functioning muscles. As it entered the lungs and combines with the oxygen and carbon dioxide in the lungs. It created a compound that caused the oxygen atoms to bond to each other and repel carbon. Causing the amount of oxygen in the lungs to jump along the lining of where oxygen was absorbed. As the carbon dioxide waste got split down, pushing the carbon to the center of the lung and at the same time, the oxygen is forced into the oxygen absorbing tissue at the sides of the lungs, causing high concentrations of oxygen at the sides without any movement of the lungs.

Then finally at the end of the first stage as the drug hits the heart and brain. It coats the heart, allowing it to beat faster without rupturing and caused the brain to send signals to the heart to speed it up. Stage two is much less complicated, the radiation given off by the drug as it

A Legend Is Born

breaks down, caused the atoms in matter to vibrate at a higher rate almost as if they were getting hotter without being hotter. This effectively slows time down for that individual. Not a huge speed difference only adding about ten seconds to how they saw each minute. However, it is just enough to give the drug the boost it needs in stage three.

This stage is the stage where it really happens, up until now the body has only been prepared for the actual speed this stage is what gives the mind the boost it needs. In the third stage the drug changes as it decayed in stage two to give off radiation. Changing the drug from a general enhancer that is triggered based on where in the body it is, to a specialized one that is focused on nerves. The drug becomes magnetized to the nerve cells in the body attaching to all of them throughout the body. Then it pushes them into overdrive. The drug not only coats and strengths the nerves, but it also increases the rate at which the signals are sent by over two hundred times. It does this by filling in any gaps a nerve has in it and the gaps in between them with a specialized coating while fixing any damage the nerves have in that process. Then, as the chemicals bound to the cells, they increase the rate at which the electric signals that flow through them travel, by over six hundred times.

Ten Thousand Walks

Once this effect hits the brain the person's mental abilities increase exponentially, allowing the person to think fast enough to move at an accelerated rate and still stay in control of their body. Combine with the first two stages the person is fully ready to use a Phantom step. In stage four the stage in which the Phantom step is used. The final part of the drug is released into the blood, this part forces the person's mind to be clear of all but one thought at a time. This allows them to have the focus needed to use the phantom style. This final part of the drug also has a time-release agent to break down all the elements of the drug leaving behind O8C2, a substance that cannot be created naturally and has a highly addictive effect on the body. In addition to the O8C2, it causes the nerve cells to break down and misfire as it leaves the blood. Causing extreme pain, problems moving, and varying twitches as the nerve cells return to the state they were in before the drug was taken. Along with the small amounts of damage the O8C2 does to every cell in the body.

This was something that I knew I wouldn't be able to fully understand anytime soon. Not only that, but from what I understood of what Paul was explaining, in order to find a counteragent that would counteract the drug safely, we would have to make a drug just as complex. Which

A Legend Is Born

Ten Thousand Walks

I knew wasn't going to be an easy task from how Paul marveled at it as if it were something so amazing and out of this world that it couldn't be from this planet.

I spent a few hours learning so many things not just about the drug, but about how many things work and interact with the body. I knew as I left that day that I had a lot to learn before I could do anything to stop the drug, but I made a vow to myself, to work on finding a way to stop it no matter how long it would take me, or what I would have to endure in order to find it.

Chapter 23: A Doctor Is Made

I began my training to be a Healer the next day. At first, it wasn't very different from when I was a child in school, just a lot of reading and studying all kinds of things. Day after day, I would hit the books so to speak and just read all day while taking notes on different things. I focused on learning everything about the human body that there was to learn.

After a few weeks of this, I got a bit tired of it, I mean I had learned a lot in a short time, but I felt as if I was getting no closer to my goal of finding a counter agent to the Shadow. Well then again, I wasn't actually working on it, but still, I felt as if all I was doing was just wasting time day after day. So, I decided that I needed to ask Paul about things, maybe he could train me and find a counter agent at the same time.

"Hey Paul, I have a question for you, it's about the drug I want you to help me find the counter agent while you train me. Or you could put off training me for a while until you find it." I said to him as he went over notes from the books he was looking through so he could give me the right one to read. *"I would totally do that, but I can't anymore. I have reached a dead end in the formula, it's*

too complex for just me to solve, so that's why I'm giving
you all this to study. I need you to be able to help me figure
this out." He said with a smile as he pulled out a book from
under the pile of books on the ground. "Got it, this is what
you need to study from back to front. Then when you're
done with that, we can finally get started with what we
need to do in order to begin working on a counter agent
that will counter the drug fully." He said then threw the
book at me.

I caught it and almost dropped it at the same time.
It was much heavier than I thought it would be, I opened
it, and the words were small, just big enough to be read.
"Wow, this is a heavy book, so I take it this book holds
everything I need to learn right." I said with a smile not
knowing what was in store for me. Paul started to laugh
at me as if I just told the funniest joke in the world. "Ahhh,
that's funny that is the first volume, the intro, you still have
A to Z, and those are much bigger than that little book."
He said with a twisted smile on his face. "You're enjoying
this aren't you?" I said back to him as I flipped through the
book to see what was in it. It made me smile for a bit when
I saw that there were pictures in it, but then I realized they
were very few of them and they had words in them too.

"Ok, I'll go study at the inn for now, I need a change of
environment." I figured I would be able to study more and

faster if I wasn't surrounded by what I still had left to do. I went back to the inn and sat in the room with the book open, I was doing my best to stay focused on it and keep reading. At first, it was easy to do, but after some time it got a lot harder to stay on track. About halfway through the day, I was about to drift off to sleep reading, then she walked in. *"Heyyyy pervert how's the studying coming along, or are you just reading about perverted things."* She said as she walked in the room looking over at the book.

"You know I have a name Annie, yep how do you like it when someone doesn't call you by your name. You don't like it do you Annie." I said, trying my best to come up with a better name than Annie, but I couldn't, I just wasn't that good at coming up with stuff like that, and it showed. She started to laugh as she dropped down on the bed on her back. *"Annie is that the best you got really. Hmm, well I actually like it, it's cute like me, and it fits me. Soooo..., tell me what you are studying now lover boy."* She said as she twirled her hands through her hair. *"The building blocks of all things, is what I'm studying."* I answered.

She didn't say anything back to me, I didn't even hear anything from her for a while. I looked up from the book, and she was just glaring at me. I looked at her confused by what she was looking at. She just smiled and rolled over and closed her eyes. *"Your nice you know that, and*

Ten Thousand Walks

I'm sorry for all the trouble I put you threw I promise I will repay you any way I can just name it." She said catching me by surprise and leaving me speechless. *"Well, I would say you can help me study, but I don't think you know anything about this stuff to help me anyway."* I answered her after being left speechless for a few minutes.

"You know I wanted to be a teacher when I was younger, I even started to train to become one. But it's just my luck that my life changed and went in a different direction than what I wanted when I was a young child." She said to me with a smile as she got up off the bed and looked down at the book in my hands to see what I was reading. She then kissed my forehead and jumped up off the bed, then ran out of the room as if she was late for something. This left me very confused, I mean what was going on here, why did she do that, was she trying to get me to stop studying.

I sat there for about twenty minutes reading and wondering what just happened, then the door opened, and she walked in. *"Ok, it's time for us to get you studying the way you need to. No more slacking off."* She said with a smile as she stood in front of me with her hands on her hips. Then she pulled the book from my hands and opened it to the very back. *"When I was studying I learned a perfect way to study that made everything go much faster, and from that look you had earlier, I know that this is just one of many books you have to study. We are going to study my way, and that is to start from the back. I learned that if I studied from the end first by the time I got halfway to the front I understood almost everything, and it just got easier as I got closer to the begging. So, let's get started pervert. Oh, and I'll even give you a reward if you go fast enough."* She said then handed me back the book and sat on the bed in front of me pointing at the book with a rod in her hand.

From then on, I did things her way, day after day we studied together, the time went by quickly as I learned faster than ever before. The days turned into weeks, then months, I got closer to finding a counter drug with each passing day. Though at times it seemed as though I would never find one and I might as well just give up, but I didn't. Mostly because she was right there reminding me of what I would be saving and slapping some sense into me when I talked about giving up.

Almost a year passed by, it felt like a blink of an eye, I had read every book in Paul's library and was moving on to the other top Healer's books. Yet still the correct formula eluded me, but with each book, I got a bit closer, soon I would find it.

A year to the day after we arrived in the city, I had

what I thought was the counter agent, but I wasn't sure if she would survive taking it. So, I did the only thing I knew to do in order to test something dangerous, I would test it on myself and see what would happen.

First, I had to actually use Shadow to see if the counter agent would have the desired effect. What's more, I had to get addicted to Shadow to see if what I made would stop the addiction or become something else that the person would get addicted to. Either way, it was still better than the Shadow I hoped it didn't have any side effects and if it did, I assumed they wouldn't be nearly as bad.

"How long did it take you to get addicted to Shadow, how many times did you take it before you knew you were addicted to it?" I asked Annabella. *"After I didn't take it on time the second time, I realized I couldn't go without it. The first time I missed taking it, I just hurt like there was no tomorrow, but it wasn't until after that when I got more and ran out again that it was bad. That time it didn't just hurt, but I started seeing and hearing things, all I could think about was when was the next time I would get more Shadow. Then, once I had enough for a week, I felt different. Every day as I got close to the time I would need to take it, I felt on edge and uneasy, as if my whole body was off."* She replied to me as the look on her face changed to one of pain, I could tell she didn't like talking

about it maybe that's why I had never heard her talk about it before.

I took one of the vials, and then went bottoms up with it, within seconds I could feel it working. My body began to tense up as I felt my breathing slow, my mind slowly began to work faster and faster. Then things around me began to look as if they were moving slower. At first, it was just a bit slower, and then it started to slow down a lot more as if time was slowing down all around me.

It was amazing how things looked all around me, I could understand why this would get addictive. The next day I took it on time like I was supposed to after this dose I wouldn't take it again until I went through withdrawal. I felt normal that day the effects were not as noticeable, but that was only because I was starting to get used to it as she said I would. *"It's been a day already, why hasn't it started to wear off yet?"* I asked Paul that night, as I stretched, then sat down in the chair for him to take some of my blood. He took a sample of my blood and put it under the microscope to take a look at it. After a few minutes of him looking at my blood and comparing it to Annabella's he spoke. *"Well, that's interesting, it seems as though the version we made is just a tiny bit stronger than the original. Maybe it's because we have a better mixing system here to mix it better."* I smiled, this was the first thing I made that he complimented. *"Well, it's better made, but the drug will still have the same effect as the original, the side effects of withdrawal should kick in later tonight, maybe in the morning we just have to wait and see. From what I can tell your vision just last longer."* He said laying back in his chair with a smile. *"Ok, that sounds good I think I'll go and get some rest and see what happens tomorrow."* I Replayed to him then got up out of the chair and headed to the door.

I left and I was delighted, even though I wasn't looking forward to the incredible pain I would be in soon. I didn't care because what I made was better than the original and that meant that I was on my way to becoming a real Healer and finding an anti-drug to the Shadow. I smiled, laying in bed for the night. I closed my eyes and drifted off to sleep.

"AHHH!!!" My screams woke everyone in the inn, Annabella jumped up and grabbed on to me. *"Are you ok, what's wrong?"* She said while looking around the room to see if there was anyone there that had attacked me. Then, as she looked back to me, she saw blood running from my eyes. *"I need more now it's ripping me apart inside."* I managed to hold back my screams long enough to speak, then I started screaming again. She grabbed the closest bottle, then held my mouth open as she poured it in. Then she held me down as I started to shake. *"Come on don't*

die on me, you said you wouldn't leave me ever, you can't do this to me." She said with tears in her eyes as I stopped breathing.

"No, you're not leaving me, I won't let you." Her crying voice said as she hit my cheeks over and over again, yelling at me to wake up. She cried and screamed the longer I wouldn't wake up. *"Wake up you pervert, I love you."* She said as she collapsed on my chest crying. *"Please wake up please."* She said crying as Paul came rushing into the room to see what was going on. He pulled her back, as she kicked and screamed at him to let her go. *"Stop, he's still alive, he just needs to wake back up I promise you he will be ok, now can you stand back while I tend to him."* He said, calming her down a little, then walking over to the bed and with a quick move stabbing me in the chest with a needle, injecting what was in it and pulling it out. A few seconds later, I jumped up screaming. *"Ahhh, what is wrong with you, why would you stab me in the heart. And why does my chest hurt so much."* I said shacking and holding my hand over my chest. I turned, and I saw Annabella by the door laughing with tears in her eyes. *"You big headed pervert trying to trick me."* She said with a smile and ran out the door.

"What just happened here?" I asked Paul still rubbing my chest. *"Nothing, how are you feeling?"* He answered

me. *"I feel fine except for my heart and chest feeling like someone was playing the drums on them."* I said back to him dropping back down on the bed. He just smiled and left the room.

The next morning, I felt like normal again the drug was flowing through my system, and I felt it. I knew I needed it now. I figured that because of how much stronger it was than the original that it must be much more addictive. Which was just what I needed to test the anti-drug. Though I figured after last night, I might need to make it a bit stronger for the next day.

I spent the rest of the day in the lab working to make the antidrug stronger. It was a little odd though, Annabella was there with me just watching my every move all day not saying anything. I was lost as to what was wrong with her, or if I had done something to her the night before to make her mad at me. However, I didn't want to say anything I just worked on the new drug as she watched on in silence. I took the Shadow that night before I went to sleep, leaving the modified version of the anti-drug to settle for the night so I could take it in the morning.

The sun peaked into my room, waking me up, I opened my eyes and looked around for a second. I was surprised to find Annabella laying next to me and not in her own bed, but I paid it no mind, I was just ready to have

this stuff out of my system, I took the anti-drug. Then I
waited as I relaxed. I didn't have anything to do that day
besides just sit and wait to see what was going to happen.
I got up for a bit trying not to wake her and broth breakfast
back to the room for us to eat. Afterwards, I laid back
on the bed thinking about how far I had come and why
Annabella was just sitting in the chair watching me from
behind the book she was reading, just loud enough for me
to hear what she was reading. I drifted off to sleep as she
read, waking up a few times when I heard the door open
and close as she went in and out of the room.

The night came much faster than I thought it would
and I didn't even get up from where I was laying, for some
reason I felt sluggish. I looked over at the bed, and I saw
her laying there. I wondered what was wrong with her
I didn't think I did anything to her, but maybe I did, and
that's why she was acting like that and not saying anything
to me. Oh well, I figured I would ask her in the morning,
she's asleep now, or at least she's acting like she is. I could
see her taking a peek down at me every few minutes as
she pretended to sleep. I looked back up at the ceiling of
the room. I felt a bit strange, I knew the drug had worn off
already, but I didn't feel like myself. Maybe it was because
I was sleeping and laying around all day, I got up and
stretched.

Ten Thousand Walks

"Ahhh!! That hurts." I said as I stretched a bit. It wasn't as bad as the last time, but it still hurts a lot. I went to lay back down the pain started to rush through my body like a fire burning my insides. *"Hand me the bottle quickly it hurts."* I said, and she was up pouring it into my mouth by the time I was done speaking the words. I didn't question how she managed to get it to me that fast, but I was happy she did. It flowed into my blood just in time, and the pain started to go away.

"Why didn't it work, it should have worked there must be a reason why it didn't." I said aloud to myself. *"Well, it kind of did, I mean it took longer to wear off this time. Maybe next time you can work on a way to stop it from wearing off."* Annabella said as she rolled over in the bed, I just laid on the ground thinking. *"Noooo!!"* I yelled a few seconds later. *"It was just a suggestion jezz you don't have to shoot it down so hard."* She said, rolling again getting comfortable in the bed. *"No, that's it, I was looking at this wrong. The radiation is the anti-drug, and it's already built into the drug that would explain the time limit perfectly. It would also explain why my antidrug didn't work at all."* I said with excitement, then grabbed her and kissed her forehead. *"I think you just solved it."* I said then vanished from the room.

I was looking at everything all wrong, the drug was

designed to be addictive. It wasn't a side effect it was the way it was made. The O8C2 wasn't a side effect of the breaking down process it was the reason for the breaking down process. I thought the radiation that was given off was to speed the atomic structure of the person, but I was wrong well mostly wrong. The radiation did do that, but it wasn't to allow the person to move even faster instead it was so that the O8C2 couldn't form until it wore off. Because of the high levels of movement in the atoms of the person, the O8C2 compound couldn't form while the radiation was still being given off thus preventing the breakdown process.

I didn't fully understand how it worked as of yet, but I knew I was close, and thanks to the Shadow flowing through me, I was thinking and focusing much clearer than I was used to. By the end of the night, I had solved the problem and figured out just how to fix it permanently. I would take out the extra oxygen in the makeup of the shadow. So instead of O8C2 being released when the radiation stopped a different but similar compound would be released O2C3 this would solve it perfectly. Now, instead of the drug in the body being broken down and ripped out of the cells nothing would happen.

I got to work on finishing it before the day was through and I headed back to the inn with it. This time the antidrug wouldn't be something that I would drink. Instead, I would have to inject it directly into my bloodstream. I pushed it into my arm and injected it into myself, then I explain it to Paul and Annabella. What I had done lessened the amount of radioactive material in the drug and altered it just enough to make O_2C_3 instead of O_8C_2 other than that I hadn't changed anything in the Shadow. I planned to turn the drug into the anti-drug for the drug, a genius plan I thought to myself as I felt it starting to work. I began to breathe harder as it started to have the effect I wanted it to.

The drug was wearing off, but instead of O_8C_2 being created in my body to breaking down and rip the drug out of my cells, O_2C_3 was created. This was perfect, the unstable O_8C_2 that was already in my body boned with the O_2C_3 and splitting off into carbon dioxide. Then it was safely exhaled. *"See, it's working, the only thing is anyone else will need a huge dose of it to get enough in their system to counteract all of it. I will add and addictive to help the cells regrow and rebuild themselves faster to make sure it's all out of the person's system as fast as possible."* I said with a smile as Paul just looked at me shaking his head. *"Wow man, you did it you solved something that this whole village couldn't solve. Congratulations, you are by all our standards a Healer of extraordinary talent."* He said as he shook my hand.

He got up and left, then turned back as he walked through the door. *"Congratulations again on curing your first patient Healer Daniel."* I looked up at him with a smile. *"You know healer sounds so unfitting, as if I did something magical. I think I will call myself a Doctor, sounds clean."* I said back to him as he left the inn.

Ten Thousand Walks

Act IX

Chapter 24: A New Life

Ten Thousand Walks

The next day came and went quickly, I worked on getting the new drug ready looking over it carefully to make sure every part of it was the way it should be. The night came, and I was ready to give Annabella the new drug. *"Are you ready, it's time for the Shadow to meet the Light."* I said to her then got the needle ready. I looked up at her and smiled a year of work, and it was all about to pay off. I got the second needle ready and smiled as I looked at her. She sat on the side of the bed. *"I'm ready now."* She said with a nervous smile on her face. I took the first needle filled with the new drug and give her the shot. Nothing happened, it was what I wanted to happen, but I wouldn't be sure until the next day. All we could do now was sleep and see what the morning broth.

The next morning, I woke up and she was gone, the second needle filled with the enhancer to help the healing process was empty. She must have taken it before she left. I thought as I stretched, I felt something was wrong though. I had a strange feeling that something was off. She didn't come and yell at me to wake up, like she usually does every morning. I looked around the room, and it hit me that all her things were gone. *"Did she just leave like that, oh well not like there was any way we could have a life together anyway, I don't know what I was thinking."* I said to myself as I began to pack up my things to get ready to leave. *"You know I thought she was different, just maybe I could have a taste of what it would be like to have a normal life for once. Oh well guess not, now it's time to move on."* I said frustrated, and jamming all my things into a bag.

I threw my coat on and put my blades on my sides, pulled my bag over my shoulder and vanished. I appeared at the front of the inn. *"It was a nice visit, but it's time for me to get going I left something in my room for you, thanks for everything see you later."* I said to Miss May then vanished. I appeared inside of Paul's house holding a bottle in my hands. *"It worked, and this is for you, I changed the drug and took a few things out of it. This should just allow you to think faster with no side effects. Take it once a month it wears off after time on its own if you don't like the effects. I will see you later Master Paul."* I said with a smile, then vanished from his house.

I stood at the top of the centermost building in the city. *"Man, I'm going to miss this place, but I guess it's time for me to go on with my journey."* I said looking around the city one last time, then vanished, seconds later I appeared at the bottom of the volcano. I looked around, and I wondered where I wanted to go then I remember where I needed to go. I had to go back to the Forge city and stop the drug from being made altogether. I reached into my bag and stopped. *"Where is my compass?"* I felted around and pulled out the box. *"Almost scared myself for a minute."* I opened the box, and it was empty, she had taken my compass, it was the only way I could find the Forge city.

I didn't know what else to do but laugh then vanished. I moved much faster than I had before and much further than I was able to before, and in much less time. The effects of the Shadow had not completely worn off yet giving me an extra boost. I stopped and didn't even realize where I was until I saw smoke. Then it hit me where I was, I was back at the lake that me and Annabella stopped at before going to the city of the Healers. Well, this time it was just whoever was here camping and me.

I walked over to the fire slowly, doing my best not to seem like I wanted to hurt the person camping. I got up to whoever it was, and they vanished. No, I thought not again. *"That took you long enough. You had me here waiting for hours you big pervert."* I just started to laugh. *"Really, you leave me in the city, and now you're saying you were waiting for me."* I said to her as I turned around. *"Well, I left you a note that said to meet me here when you woke up."* She said, then I reached over and pulled a note from the coat pocket she was wearing. *"Oops, I guess I took the wrong coat when I left."* She said with an evil little smile. I knew she didn't take the wrong coat, but she planed it to see if I would come looking for her. *"Sure... wrong coat. And I didn't come looking for you if that's what you think I just came back this way."* I said to her then took the compass from the other pocket of the coat she was wearing.

"Oh, is that all you wanted from me, just what I had in my pockets, your horrible you know just horrible." She said pushing me back. *"Now where are we going to go from here, are we going to the Forge city or not."* She said to me and stuck her tongue out at me with her hands folded.

"We do need to go back to the Forge city, but we don't need to get there now sooo... how about we just take our time and look around as we head there. You know enjoy ourselves a bit before we get back to saving everyone else. Plus, I heard rumors about a lot of strange things happing in the city close to where we are now it could be the work of the Shadow. How about we go explore and see what we can find out." I answered her with a smile as I took her hand and pulled her along as I walked.

From there we headed through the forest in search of the next town over. Which wasn't all that far, but at a normal speed of travel, it would take us a few weeks to get there on foot. *"How about we speed things up a bit I'll even carry you."* I said to her as we walked. *"Hmm, let me think about that. No, I think you just want a reason to feel me up we can walk. Besides, what's your hurry pervert, do you have some woman there that you're rushing to get to."* I just laughed as I walked. *"No, no I don't, it's ok, we can walk I haven't really taken it easy since I started the journey to find my father so so long ago. I think you're right that we shouldn't hurry."* I said with a smile as I gazed into the bright blue skies. Something I had not done in so many years.

The next few weeks passed by quickly, as me and Annabella traveled to the closest city. What we found in the town was interesting and well not very unexpected, to say the least. We found a bunch of thugs that had found a way to get Shadow, and were using it to make money. I checked it out, and after giving them the anti-drug, I took whatever drugs they had on them and analyzed it. From what I could tell it was the same, but just a bit stronger than the other one that Annabella use to take.

It didn't take us long to find out where they got it from and from there we went. Day after day turned into week after week of us traveling and following the trails of those dealing the Shadow. We shut down dealer after dealer over the months to come, and soon we were almost back at the source of the drug the Forge city. However, for some reason, it seemed as though she didn't want to go back to the city and end all this, as if she just wanted to keep on following all these trails.

I sat looking out at the lake we had stopped by, I remember so well I was shot out of this lake after leaving the underground city. Annabella was laying with her head in my lap, playing with her hair. I looked down at her and thought about all the time we had spent together over the past two years. It hit me that over all that time I never really took some time to actually look at her. She was an amazing woman. Her long black hair flowed down to her hips like the shimmering waters of the lake in front of me. Her body was small and well built, but not too much, I could see the muscles in her hands but nowhere else. I closed my eyes and ran my fingers down her soft, smooth skin. She was the perfect woman for anyone. So why was she here with me a cursed soul wandering the earth?

"Are you scared to go to the Forge city, because it seems like you're doing everything to keep me from going there. What are you afraid of?" I asked her as my hand ran across her face. She opened her eyes and smiled at me. Taking my hand in hers and just lying there not saying anything until I was going to ask her again. *"You know you are cute when you don't understand something."* She said with a smile, then turned her head to the lake, took my hand and, pointed it to the shore of the lake. *"Look*

out there, what do you see?" She asked me, I looked up and paused, then answered her. *"I see a lake, a large one that is filled by a huge network of caves that leads to an amazing underground..."* Her finger went to my lips stopping me from finishing my sentence.

"Hush and just look at what's there what I see is possibilities, a vast lake that can become anything we choose. We can build anything here in this amazing place. It's not just what's there, it's what can be there that's important. That's why I don't want to go to the Forge city I don't want to fight I want to be happy and just live for a while. Can I have that, can you let me just live and be happy for a while please it's all I want. And if you stay here and live with me, I promise I will repay you for giving me back my life any way I can." She said then turned from looking at me when she stopped talking to look at the lake, I could see a tear in her eyes. This was a side of her I had never seen.

"I will make you a deal, the city follows a path, it's a long one, but it will be back here in about a year and a half maybe two. How about we stay here, right here on this lake, and just wait for it to come back. No more going after it, we can just wait here for it to come to us, is that ok with you." I said to her with a smile turning her head back to me. She smiled and jumped up wrapping her hands around

Ten Thousand Walks

me. *"That's ok pervert. I think I can handle that."* She said, with a voice that hid a joyful cry behind it.

The next two years showed me an entirely new side of her, and I showed her a side of myself that I thought I had lost over a hundred years ago. The days and weeks passed like a dream, filled with joy and laughter. We built a home to live in as we waited for the city to come back around. She even rescued a pet, well she called it a pet I called it a beast. A white tiger, one of the largest I had ever seen in all my travels.

The first year was the hard one, that year we had a lot to do. That was the year we built our home together, it took us almost six months of working all day almost every day to build it. Once that was done, we had to find things and places to go to get all the things we would need to live the way we wanted to.

Then after that, it was all fun and games so to speak, well at least that's how I felt. Every day I woke up to her doing something strange, making me laugh every morning as she fought to keep me from seeing what she was doing. I even had a birthday party I knew nothing about, which I had no clue how she managed to pull off when I knew where she was all the time. Well, at least I thought I knew where she was all the time anyway.

For those two years, I was happy and felt as if I

belonged for the first time in my life and it made me wish that the city would never come back around. But I knew it would be coming soon, and I was ok with it coming, though I didn't want it to.

"The city should be here in two days at most, after that it will all be over. We can finally finish what was started and get back to our life the way it should be." I said with a smile on my face, then gave her a kiss on the lips.

Chapter 25: Return Of The Shadow

The day came, and I looked out the window in our living room, I saw a cloud of smoke in the distance moving towards us, and I knew it was the Forge city. It was time to get started. I walked inside to a chest I hadn't opened since the house was built, a year and a half ago. I flipped it opened, Annabella heard it open, and she walked into the room. I pulled out a dark black cloak, then turn to look at her. *"It's time we get started, my love."* I said to her as I pulled it over my shoulders. *"Oh, looking good mister, but do you think you still had it after all this time."* She said with a smile, I smiled back. Vanished and I was behind her pulling the other coat in my hand over her shoulders. I leaned forward to her ear. *"You tell me if I still got it."* I said then kissed her on the cheek. She smiled and took my hand and walked to the door, opened it and walked out. She turned to me, smiled, kissed me then spoke. *"One more mission, our last mission, and it will all be over."* She said with a smile.

We watched as the city moved out from behind the tree line and into our view. The shadow it cast crept over us, and as it hit our dark cloaks, they blended in with it and vanished.

Ten Thousand Walks

Chapter 26: Final Shadow Shows

We appeared on the ground dead center under the city, I looked up at the main engine of the city. Its massive 300-foot turbines pulled air down from the sides of the city and pushed it out here. It wasn't what kept the city in the air, but it was what kept the city stable and always leave no matter the weather. The process of pulling air down through the city created a circulating air effect that countered the high winds around the city at that height. A spectacular design by all standers.

Nevertheless, it had just one problem. With that design and we were going to take full advantage of it. Though the design could stand up to the worst storm it had the problem of it had no fail-safe, everything in it had to run perfectly, or it didn't work at all. If the turbine slowed or sped up too much the wind around the city would go rushing through the city, or the city could lose its stability. Which was just my plan, I would use my Air Blades to cut a few parts in the turbine. Very minuscule parts, but just enough to slow the turbine down about three rotations per minute. Not sufficient enough to destabilize the city, but enough to prevent the wind countering that the turbines generated. Meaning the city was about to get very windy.

Ten Thousand Walks

"Ready to get started sweetheart?" I asked with a smile. *"Yes, just lead the way, and I will follow you Hun."* She answered, and then looked up at the turbine. She was waiting for me to make the first move, it was time I got started with my plan to send the city into chaos. Then, use it as cover so we could enter the city without having to fight.

I looked over at her, then up at the turbine above. I drew my blades, then I vanished appearing just under the center of the turbine engine. Two quick slashes through the casing and then one stab into the engine controller box, before I started to fall back to the ground.

With a flip, I landed on the ground feet first like a feather. *"Should take about two minutes before the engines slow. Without the controller, there will be nothing to speed it back up. Once it has slowed enough, we will be heading up to get started."* I said to her with a smile.

Our cloaks flowed in the wind as the city's turbines slowly passed from directly over our heads. *"Let's get this started babe."* I said with a smile then vanished. I appeared on top of one of the massive blade railings of the turbines. My legs hung off it balancing me as I leaned forward, reaching out with my right hand while my left hand held onto the railing below me. I closed my fingers and as I did her hand appeared in mine, I winked at her. She just nodded at me, and I moved, pulling her up and sending her straight up between two of the blades and through the small shaft to the top of the city.

She flew up and out of the small opening at the cities underground leave, then just as she started to fall I appeared with my hands under her. *"The wind is picking up, the alarm for the air controls should be going off any second, and once it does no one will notice the intruder alarm we will be setting off once we move again."* I said as we stay perfectly still my feet jammed against the walls of the hole we came through. The sensors don't set off any alarms unless what comes in here moves and has a heat signature, and seeing that the cloaks prevented most of the heart in our bodies from showing up on the sensors we would be fine if we didn't move again.

BEEP WHOA BEEP!! The sound of the air control alarm went off. With that, we vanished, appearing at the top of the builds throughout the city, then disappearing again almost the same time. We had to find the new lab. Which means we need to find a large building, with enough ventilation and closed off windows to block out the light. We found the only building that the drug could be made in and appeared in front of it. No one noticed the two of us standing there in front of the building with all the confusion from the alarms. We looked around to find a way in then we just vanished, leaving behind and after image that looked only like two shadows that quickly disappeared when the light hitting them.

We appeared at the top of the building near a ventilation shaft, and with one quick swing, the top of it came flying off. With another quick movement I jumped in, she followed right behind me jumping over the side of the vent and into it. I came crashing through the other end of the vent in the ceiling of the inside of the lab. Going through the vent cap and landing on one of the tables on one knee. I looked up to see that I was surrounded by lab techs I smiled, stood to my feet, and held my hands out as Annabella fell right into my hands.

"I will make this easy on you, just go now, and I won't hurt you, sound good?" I said with a smile, hoping they would just give up and go, so I didn't have to waste any of my time fighting. My hopes were torn down though. They all smiled as if I was just some random theft. *"Who do you think you are, breaking in this place like you are so powerful."* Said the person that looked like the lead scientists with a big smirk on his face. I looked at him and smiled, then put Annabella to stand next to me. *"Go ahead and take it, I think these guys have something up their sleeves."* I said to Annabella

She smiled and pulled the version of the Shadow that

I had made as a cure from her coat, she popped the top off and drunk it. Then dropped the glass and as it fell, I turned to kiss her as the leader spoke again. *"We created that drug do you really think we have never taken it."* The leader said in anger as we kissed ignoring him completely, making him even angrier. *"I'll show you why you shouldn't ignore me."* He said then vanished, his fist went straight through our after image.

   "Do you really think you can hit me moving that slow." I said with a smirk on my face from across the room. He stumbled as he tried to catch himself from falling off the table. I could see the shock in their eyes when they turned to me. I just continued to talk. *"Well, how about now, do you just want to give up and not get hurt?"* I said, then walked from where I was standing towards the center of the room. He jumped off the table.

   "Got you." He said, giving a signal to the others that were in the lab with us. They all pulled weapons and aimed them at me. *"Your first mistake was letting us see her drink the shadow, your second mistake was not drinking it yourself. And your last and biggest mistake was walking away from her."* He said with a smile, I just looked at him and laughed. *"Think your smart cause you took it already. Well, guess what even with the Shadow you won't be able to dodge the arrows at the speed these are shot."* He said

again with a lot of pride and boosting in his voice. I knew he was the one that designed them, which meant this was going to be fun to watch him react to me catching them. I started laughing and raised my hand gesturing for him to come.

He snapped when I started laughing. *"Kill him! All of you, fire I want his blood everywhere."* He yelled, pulling his weapon out and aiming it at me. I stopped laughing as they all started firing. My phantom turned into copies appearing everywhere catching all the arrows, then vanishing letting the arrows hit the ground. *"Your first mistake was not leaving when I gave you a chance to. Your second mistake was thinking my lovely companion here was the one moving me. And your last and dumbest mistake was thinking I take that nonsense you call Shadow."* I said with a sinister smile on my face.

They all vanished, coming after me just as I finish speaking. I moved as phantom copies of myself sent them flying back. Then I looked over at Annabella and nodded my head at her, she vanished. It was going exactly as I planned, I would hold them off while she destroyed the drug in the main lab, and add the additive that I design over the two years to the rest. The additive would add the extra compound to the drug to turn it into mine, turning it into a cure that would stop the addiction.

Ten Thousand Walks

They turned their attention to her. *"No, you don't, your fight is with me, and I don't think you have time to be taking your eyes off me."* I said, pulling their attention back to me as my phantom copies began to appear all around them. This time I had their full attention and I was going to teach them a lesson. My phantoms moved in on them quickly dealing them one blow after the other so fast they could hardly keep track of my phantoms.

They attacked all at once shooting and punching as fast as they could, but it was all useless, they were just hitting the phantoms after I had already moved. Then I just knock them back and rough them up a bit to make it seem as if that's all I could do because I was at my limit and just barely keeping myself from getting hurt. This way they would focus on me alone and forget about Annabella as she changed the formula that they wrote for the drug to mine and adding my additive to the ones they had already made.

It only took her about a minute to do then the part of the plan that made this all fit together was next. She would destroy the lab and some of the drug, once she started to destroy the lab it was time for the big performance. I let one of the arrows hit me in the shoulder bouncing off the coat as another one grazed my ear. I jumped back as explosions went off in the lab.

Ten Thousand Walks

"Let's go, Annabella we did enough damage already, it's time for us to get out of here." I said with my hand to the ear that was hit by the arrow, doing my best to sound as if I was hurt badly. "We're not going to let you get away from us that easy." The leader said. I just looked at him with an angry look as Annabella appeared next to me. Then we both vanished.

We appeared at the top of the building where the vent was with a smile on our faces, we had done it as planned, and nothing went wrong. "Let's get out of here baby, the rest of the plan will be done by them without us needing to lift a finger." I said laughing. I took her hand in mine, and we vanished from the top of the city. Appearing at the far end where they kept the carriers. "Hey boys long time no see." I said with a smile, then turned to the control tower. I knew Adam would be inside, after all, it was where I went to go find him when I lived here.

I looked up at the window, then appeared in front of it, with a smile on my face taunting him. Then I took it a bit further, I pulled my blades out, and in a flash, I cut the entire top of the control tower off. I landed on the ground below the tower. With a sick smile on my face, they didn't know I hand cut the top off as of yet. I looked over at Annabella and nodded for her to go, she vanished appearing on the top of the watchtower then vanishing again. I appeared in front of the tower one last time, I grabbed onto the side of the tower just above where I had cut, then I pushed my feet against the tower as I pulled on the top. The top began to move, then the glass all around the cut shattered and the top began to come crashing down into the control room I glanced over at Adam then vanished.

Minutes later we were back at the house we had built happy our plan went just as we planned there was no way they would figure out the plan we had come up with. We walked to the door of our house with a smile on our faces it was time for us to retire theses cloaks for good this time.

"How long do you think it will take before they realize what we did babe?" I said to her as I reached for the door. *"It doesn't matter it's done."* She replied, pulling my hand from the door and kissed me slowly. I paused to enjoy the moment, then I reached for the door. BOOM. The house exploded, sending us flying back.

I hit the ground, jumping up and turned to her to see if she was ok, I was relieved that she looked unharmed. The cloaks must have taken most of the impact of the blast. Thank God for that. I thought as I got up and picked her up. She looked at me. *"What was that, where did it come from."* She said her voice shaking as she spoke. *"Don't worry I thought they might attack, but I didn't think* they would be this bold to do it after I took out their control center. Guess I was wrong, well let's show them a thing or two about what we can do." I said to her hugging her, and then turning to the city as waves of carriers flew from the city.

I held her hand then pulled her in wrapping my hand around her body, then I moved taking her with me. I headed for a clearing that was a few miles away, maybe they wouldn't be able to track me there.

I stopped stumbling in the valley just under the volcano where the city of the healers was. I looked around behind me to see if they were still coming, thinking I had lost them, but I was wrong they were right there flying right for us. *"Man, these guys don't give up at all but how did they even find us."* I said to her as I pulled my blades out and turned to face the oncoming waves of Carriers. *"Just wait here for a bit I'm going to cut them down to size."* I said to Annabella then vanished, I appeared in between the oncoming Carriers and let loses.

Slash after slash, my hand sent my blades through the Carriers one after the next. I was hitting one, then using it to jump off of, vanishing as I passed through others and stopping as I hit another. Then sending the blades down between my legs into the carrier I was on top of, then off I went again to the next one. I flew from carrier to carrier, like a tornado ripping them to pieces as I moved in-between them.

I reappeared next to Annabella and leaned over to catch my breath, I hadn't fought like that in two years, I had lost a bit of my edge and needed some time to catch my breath back before I got started again. I estimated they would be on top of us by the time I was finished catching my breath, then I will end this I thought to myself as I gasped for air.

I looked up as they flew overhead, raining down weapons fire from above. I vanished with Annabella, we appeared in the air, and I swung her around then threw her through the air. She flew by the Carriers slashing at them as she passed, leaving a trail of explosions in the air behind her. Like lines of fire through the air. I dropped back to the ground, then vanished pulling her out of the air and back to the ground. We looked up as the carrier's dropped soldiers.

"Looks like they figured out that if they stayed up there, they would just be sitting ducks for us to pick off." I said laughing as the troops began to land. I looked over at Annabella with a winked, then vanished. I appeared in front of the troops. "You can't win. You've already seen what I can do so why not just give up already." I said to them with my blades in hand. They looked at me as if I was joking and with a smile, they vanished. This I saw coming, and I vanished stopping them in their tracks as I sent them flying back. Then Annabella joined me.

We started to fight back to back vanishing and appearing all over as we fought laying waste to the army that grew more and more as they closed in on us. We had the advantage, there was no way we could lose with our speed. Arrows began to fly through the air, my smile grew as I caught them out of the air, cutting some and then cutting through their weapons before they could reload to fire again. I appeared next to Annabella with a smile, she was breathing hard. *"Relax for a minute I'll take care of things babe."* I said to her. Then the sun disappeared behind a dark cloud. I looked up, and it was arrows blanketing the sky above us.

They came falling down on us, and I moved, I vanished, and my phantom copies appeared all around her. Catching and deflecting every arrow that was coming to her. The copies disappeared as the light from the sun hit them. I appeared next to her and helped her back up. *"Ready to finish this?"* WHOOSH.

I vanished and appeared in the army and went crazy slashing at their weapons destroying and hurting them but not killing anyone. A few minutes later, I reappeared next to Annabella. *"Are you going to help me finish dealing with* them?" I said with my back to her watching them close in on us. *"I'm so sorry baby."* The words were hiding pain on the edge of crying. I turned, she was sitting with her hand on her stomach. Blood running out from between her fingers.

DOOOM!! The sound of something crashing in the distance echoed as I realized she had been hit with an arrow. I rushed forward and held her. *"You will be ok baby just relax I will get you to the healers they will fix you up just hold on."* I said with tears running down my face, holding her close. *"I wish I had met you earlier, but its ok, I love you. You made me so happy these past three years."* She said, the pain fading from her voice and beginning to get weaker. *"No baby save your strength you will be ok, don't talk like you're not going to be ok."* I said, my voice breaking with my tears. *"I love you, my pervert, I love you so much never forget that."* Her words faded.

I felt no heartbeat from her. I pulled her to me and held her tight. *"NO baby don't leave me, I love you too I need you!"* I yelled out as my tears ran down my face, followed by screams. *"AHHHHHHHHHHHHHHH!!"* I dropped down to my knees with her in my hands leaning over her crying. The troops came closing in on all sides. They smiled as the huge army surrounded me mocking my pain.

Chapter 27: Ten Thousand

Ten Thousand Walks

My tears flowed down my face slowly, burning like knives as they flowed down my cheek. Setting my heart ablaze with anger and pain, my rage built as the army inched in towards me. I just wanted them to all die for what they had done. My mind went blank as the tears reached my chin. Moments later the army got ready for their attack. They stepped in close surrounding me in a circle. Twenty of them took aim, as my tears fell from my chin.

My tears fell all in one drop. It moved slowly as if time was slowing down to mourn her death with me. The instant my tears hit her body my blades were already through the men that were closing in on me. The image of me holding Annabella disappeared, and it was replaced by phantom copies all with blades threw the ones surrounding me. They couldn't believe it, they were just about to fire on me, and now my blades were running through their bodies. Then, before they could do anything, the phantom faded, and I lost my mind with anger and pain.

Moving through the army laying waste to them as thousands of phantoms appeared and disappeared. Cutting the army down by the thousands every second. My phantoms grew in number as my rage grew, I lost myself in my anger. My heart pumped adrenaline through my veins, pushing me to move faster and put more strength into every move. I began to push the number of phantom copies I have ever made, surpassing my previous limit by the thousands.

My mind started to go blank as an overwhelming amount of rage flooded through every aspect of my mind, overflowing from my mind into my very soul. I screamed out in anger, and sorrow, my very soul, raging against all that was. I could no longer hold myself together, I lost all control of who I was, I became more animal than anything else, my rage rushed out of my heat and into my blood. It boiled hotter as my eyes blurred with tears. Then I attacked with every bit of strength I had, attacking everything I saw in my path.

Within minutes the army was gone, all that was left was a field filled with bloody bodies. I stood still filled with rage and anger, not knowing what to do next, I had no one left to kill, but I was still filled with rage. I fell to my knees and cried out in pain, weeping my very heart out. I was alone again, and I didn't want to be alone again the pain was too much for me. Click! I heard something behind me, then a footstep. My mind blanked out again, it was time to destroy again.

I moved appearing in front of a tall man, my knives were deflected away from him without me even noticing.

Ten Thousand Walks

I looked down his hands had moved perfectly to let him block me with almost no effort. I swung again bringing my blades around, heading straight for his head. There was no way he could dodge my attack, no one could.

I stumbled into him a bit my blades only cutting his hair. *"Clam down Daniel my..."* I stopped him, I moved both my arms right to his stomach and heart. I moved with all my force and speed even though he tried to block it my knives went straight into him. Ripping through his body and out his back. I held him up in the air with his feet almost a foot off the ground, he struggled for a few moments then his body just went motionless.

I dropped him and stepped back slowly, I looked at what I had just done. From the army that was laying all around me down to the person laying on the ground with my blades sticking out of his chest. I fell to my knees and screamed out. *"Oh, can you stop being so loud, I'm already in pain I don't need my head hurting too you know."* A voice came from in front of me. I looked up, and he was standing in front of me, with both my blades still sticking out of him.

He grabbed both of them and quickly pulled them from his body. As they left his body, the blood on them was drawn back into the wounds just before they closed. Then his clothes repaired itself as he leaned forward to

A Legend Is Born

me. *"Please relax I'm not one of these guys, I didn't have anything to do with the death of your beloved. I truly feel for you so please don't do that again, it hurts you know."* He said then handed my blades back to me.

I took them and then vanished appearing behind him with my blades to his neck. *"Who are you, what are you, and how do you know my name?"* I asked, pulling my blade just to touch his neck. My questions were met by laughter as he stepped forward. My blade went through his neck as if it were air. He then turned to me with a smile and not a mark on his neck. *"Your funny Danny boy, I know everything about you, your mind is like an open book to me. My name is Will or William, whichever you want to call me they are both my names. And those silly little things, though they are very sharp, they can't kill me."* He said pointing to my blades and then walked around me. *"It also looks as if you are like me in a way, seems as though you will never know death yourself too."* He continued to talk.

I looked at him, shocked but still very angry, and filled with so much pain because of what had just happened. *"That's great for you now remove yourself from my path I have something to do."* I said to him as I pushed him out of the way. *"You know destroying the city won't fix what happened. It was only the work of a few that did this to you. Why not just punish them in a way that would be worse than death? After all, we are both men of unusual power, and we know that they are things worse than death."* He said with an evil tone as if he enjoyed the suffering of others.

For a moment, I was beginning to create a plan to destroy them. Then a voice in my head spoke as though it was the voice of someone else. *"Is this what you spent all those years searching for?"* I looked around at Will, he was just smiling as if he knew what the voice in my head was saying. Then he spoke shocking a little sense into me. *"Well, tell me is this what you searched all these years for. Is this what you wanted to become a destroyer or a saver, because from where I stand you are a destroyer that makes even me the man who caused the destruction of his own race, look like a man of peace."* His words calmed and shocked me at the same time. What was going on?

"You humans are all the same no matter what planet you're from." He said as he walked away from me. I watched him then I turned to the city, I just couldn't let them go to keep doing what they were, but I couldn't Kill them all it wouldn't be right, and I would become a monster if I did that.

With my anger raging over in my mind, I moved. I appeared under the city and then vanished. I flew up the main engines vent slashing my blades through everything as I went up. Then, as I fell I aimed my blades straight down and cut right through the turbine. I hit the ground, and the turbine exploded above me, the city started to come down. The open valley that I was in was close by, close enough for the city to just reach as it hit the ground.

I was to protect this great city from what might destroy it even if what I was protecting it from was itself. I vanished and appeared at one of the four outer engines, in a flash I sent my blades through it hundreds of times, and it fell to pieces. I repeated this on all four outer engines, then I sat looking at the final one as the pieces burned. I hope they learn their lesson by the time they get it all fixed. I thought to myself staring into the flames of the engine.

"See that wasn't too hard and no one else got hurt." Will's voice came from behind me, I didn't even see or hear him walk up to me, but there he was with a smile on his face. *"Yeah, I might have made their lives a little bit harder over the next few months while they replace the broken engines, but in the long run I really haven't done anything, they will just rebuild and remake the drug, then it will all start over again."* I said to him as I gazed off into the skies wondering if I made the right choice.

"Don't worry yourself so much, how about we be friends, after all, we will be alive for a very long time might

as well have someone to talk to once in a while right. And I
think you could use a hand in making up for the amount of
lives you took here today. Maybe you could use some help
finding a way to keep these things from happening again."
He said to me as he walked around the burning engines,
picking at parts of it. I looked over at him thinking, he
must not be all there. However, if he could find a way to
fix it so, the people in this city couldn't hurt anyone again,
without hurting anyone in the city; I would consider being
his friend. I thought to myself watching him fiddle with the
parts he was poking at.

"*Well, say no more I know just what to do.*" He said as
if he was right there in my head, listening to my thoughts.
Then, as I was about to speak, he walked away from me.
"*What is wrong with this guy?*" I said to myself as he
walked up to the edge of the city and placed his hand on
the broken engine, closing his eyes and just standing still as
if waiting for something. "*Hey come now there is nothing
wrong with me, and I'm doing what you wanted, a way of
stopping them without killing them.*" A voice in my head
spoke to me sounding just like Will, but it couldn't be he
was too far away for me to hear.

"*Man, humans are not as smart as I thought, you
know for someone that's over 200 years old you sure are
dumb. You can hear me because I am here in your mind

you fool. For a person that can't die no matter what it should be easy for you to believe that a person like me is real." The voice said again in my head. I looked over at him and wondered if he could read minds.

What's he doing over there and how is this going to stop anything. *"Ah, but you see only with your eyes, you see not only can I see into your mind and the minds of others but I can see into machines as well. However, there is a bit of a difference with machines I can control what they do. In this case, I can cause them to destroy themselves, preventing any of the systems in this city from working again. By doing this, they will have to rebuild everything in the entire city from the ground up."* His voice continued in my head, then something else I didn't expect came into my mind. A strange sight and feeling at the same time, of the people in the city. I could see and feel how they did things and I could see that with all the technology in the city destroyed, they would never be able to rebuild it, they would have to become an ordinary village. This meant the end of their technological control of others. I smiled this meant that I would have justice, and at the same time, I would not be harming them, but I would be protecting them from themselves.

Will walked up to me and smiled. *"I have a question for you, and your answer to it is very important."* He said to me with a smile I just nodded and waited for him to ask. *"Well, I have seen what you have done here. Your power is amazing beyond anything I have ever seen. So, are you going to be a destroyer and destroy all that gets in your way, is that the reason for your power?"* He asked me, which left me a bit shocked, I didn't think someone would ask a question like that after what I had just done. *"Well, I know what I did, but I was born to protect others, I have gained all these skills to do just that, but now I no longer have a reason to do it."* I said to him with pain in my voice.

   "Daniel, is strong and powerful and your name will go down in history as the most destructive person who ever lived, but is that what you want." He said to me. I looked at him and confused by how he spoke, but I understood it and wondered if I want to be known for destruction, or did I want to be a savior. *"No, I want to be a person that saves others."* I said to him. He smiled at me and then closed his eyes. *"You can no longer go by the name Daniel, that is a human name. I think it is best that you go by something else. Something powerful, something that brings hope and something that will ring through the ages. Well, you can pick a name in a while. For now, I have something for you to help you decide. Close your eyes and open your mind."* He said to me, confusing me a bit. His words were somewhat random there was no real logic behind them.

250   *A Legend Is Born*

Ten Thousand Walks

As I was thinking about what he said, I felt a strange feeling of love. Overwhelming my mind and pushing out all of the anger and pain. I opened my eyes and looked at him, he just smiled. I didn't understand what this feeling was then I felt something very familiar. *"Aw, come on, don't you get it by now I'm giving you the greatest gift, the last thoughts and feelings of the one you loved so much."* He said closing his eyes as his face got more serious, what I felt at that point was beyond words.

My mind was lost I couldn't tell how much time was passing all I could feel was Annabella's love engulfing me completely. Then I heard her voice, it was faint at first and wasn't speaking words, but I understood what she was saying somehow. She was happy, so happy that she got to spend the last two years together peacefully. I had saved her from the life that was destroying who she was, and I gave her a life that was filled with joy. I smiled and fell to my knees weeping with joy.

Will opened his eyes and spoke. *"She loved you to the very end and didn't blame you for anything, and I have something to tell you, that she wanted you to know that you might not have been able to understand. She wanted to tell you that you gave her so many reasons to be happy and she wanted to do the same for you."* I looked up at him smiling.

Ten Thousand Walks

"What did you mean by I need a name that carried my power with it." I asked. *"Pick a name that will carry your power with you and not just anger."* He replied. *"But I have none that I can think of I just want to leave this place and be done with it all."* I said back to him. It was silent for a while, then he smiled as if he figured out something. He walked over to Annabella's body I turn to see what he was doing. He leaned over her and as he moved her coat to the side, I drew my blades and attacked him. Running them right through him. *"Get away from her you don't have the right to touch her!!"* I yelled at him, he just grabbed onto something she had with her as I lifted him with my blades and threw him across the field.

He hit the ground, and I appeared above him as he landed, my blades headed straight for his neck. He held up a piece of paper in his hand to defend himself. *"Wait, she was going to give this to you after the fight."* I stopped right as my blades were going to go through the paper. I held one blade to his neck as I took the paper from him. It had one line on it.

"You gave me Ten Thousand reasons to love you when I only needed one."

I put away my blades and reached down to help Will back up. *"I think I know what name I'm going to use now."* I said to him as he dusted himself off. He just smiled

A Legend Is Born

Ten Thousand Walks

"Well then my new friend shall we give her the Burial she deserves." He said to me walking back to her body.

We stood at her grave looking at the tombstone I had made for her. *"My first love, the one that taught me the meaning of the word love and showed me what was worth fighting for, I will miss you for the rest of time, and I will honor you by saving all those who need to be saved."* I said then turned to Will, looked at him for a second then just walked away. *"Hey, wait up, where are you going?"* Will said as he walked behind me. I looked back at him. *"People need saving out there, and I'm going to go save them."* I said as I walked away from he followed me.

He walked behind me quietly for a few minutes. I looked back as I walked, wondering what he was doing following me. I was going to ask what he was doing behind me, but he spoke before I could. *"I'm coming with you of course. After all, you can't save the world alone Daniel, or should I say Ten Thousand."* I smiled a bit and glanced back at him, then I replied to him. ***"Will and Ten Thousand the Cursed Heroes saving the universe, Hmm, I do like the sound of that."***

A Legend Is Born   **253**

Thank you for coming on this wondrous adventure with me.
I hope you enjoyed reading it as much as I enjoyed writing it.

More books in the Cursed Heroes series

Loaded -Ebook: 978-1-7359149-3 Print: 978-1-7359149-2-3

Cold As Ice – Ebook: 978-1-7359149-4-7 Print: 978-1-7359149-5-4

Other Books available at: Mowuniverse.com/store

See you in the next adventure